Praise f

... a compe   , ...

careful atte......u... ..u ....storical detail. The women's stories are moving, and readers will come away wanting to know this Jesus they describe.

Editor at The Writers Edge

Blending disciplined imagination with a sensitive reading of biblical stories, Merikay McLeod gives us well-wrought portraits of women who loved Jesus and whom Jesus loved. With steady pacing, she takes us through shock, suffering, grief and memory to unbelievable joy. Her story offers integrity for encountering Easter.

Dr. Phyllis Trible
University Professor of Biblical Studies
(emerita) at Wake Forest University
Divinity School and Baldwin Professor
of Sacred Literature (emerita) at Union
Theological Seminary in New York,
as well as past president of the Society of
Biblical Literature.

A poignant new insight on the death and resurrection of Christ told by the women who loved him.

Antoinette May
Author of the New York Times bestseller
Pilate's Wife.

The Day After His Crucifixion is a psalm of mourning and remembrance. Like a wake, the women most affected by Jesus' ministry tell their own stories of how he impacted their lives. Following the narrative, author Merikay McLeod provides discussion questions connecting readers with the book's themes, reminding us that we are sisters in grief.

> Nancy Werking Poling
> Author of *Had Eve Come First and Jonah Been a Woman*

Rich in biblical allusions and symbolism, ... the standout to me is McLeod's focus on the gathering of women to share memories of Jesus, a communal space for women where storytelling reinforces faith and offers comfort. Although the outcome is well-known, the journey to get there is both powerful and affecting, beautifully conveyed through McLeod's skillful writing.

> Jamie Michele
> Readers' Favorite Reviews

The originality of *The Day After His Crucifixion* is distinct in the genre of biblical literature. This book is more than a depiction of Christian love .... It is a sensitive and telling affirmation for believers and a compelling introduction to understanding what Christianity means.

> Constance Stadler
> Readers' Favorite Reviews

THE DAY AFTER HIS
CRUCIFIXION

THE DAY AFTER HIS CRUCIFIXION

Women who followed Yeshua the Nazarene grapple
with the horror of his execution

A Biblical Novella

Merikay McLeod

Published by Front Porch Publishing
Mountain Home, North Carolina

Distributed by Gatekeeper Press
7853 Gunn Hwy., Suite 209
Tampa, FL 33626
www.GatekeeperPress.com

Library of Congress Control Number: 2024951225

ISBN (paperback): 9781662955518
eISBN: 9781662955525

Dedicated to
Kit Watts
(1943 - 2023)

Kit's love for Yeshua and her support of
other women following His Way
is a living inspiration.

CONTENTS

PREFACE AND ACKNOWLEDGEMENTS

In the 1970s, while taking classes in the Women's Studies Program at San Jose State University, I began thinking about all the women who were active in the life of Jesus, from his mother to his many friends and followers including the dozens of unnoticed women who provided funds and (no doubt) food for him and his band of disciples. If they were to share the experiences they had with Jesus, what would they say? What details about him would they notice and remember?

Twenty years later, while studying for my master's degree in Spirituality at Santa Clara University, I was still thinking about all those women we have never met, but who were as real as the disciples.

About the turn of the century I realized that many of my professional friends and associates, those a decade or so younger than I am, knew virtually nothing about Jesus' life and mission. They were curious but weren't interested in attending church or reading a Bible to learn more. They asked me questions and I did my best to answer or to point them to books on the subject.

Eventually my thinking and imagining, along with my studying and researching turned into the desire to write a book telling the story of Jesus. It would not be a religious or theological study but a collection of stories. Women's stories. I'd use Jesus' native name, "Yeshua," rather than the English translation of "Jesus." I'd do my best to give voice to the women involved, letting them describe their life-altering experiences with the Son of Man/Son of God.

Over the years, from northern California to the Blue Ridge Mountains of North Carolina, I have worked and re-worked this manuscript of stories. Many others have contributed to my efforts.

My dear friends Kit Watts and Dr. Penny Shell were among the first readers of my earliest draft. Their encouragement kept me focused on these New Testament women.

Christian literary agent, Leslie Stobbe assured me that women of all ages would find this novella intriguing and inspirational. He suggested adding study questions to the manuscript.

Members of my writers group — poet Ann Greenleaf Wirtz, novelist Leanna Sain, and inspirational author Karin Wooten — contributed suggestions that helped tighten and sharpen my writing.

Donna Radich applied her English teacher skills to the manuscript's punctuation, removing errant commas, adding semicolons where appropriate, and in general "cleaning up" the text.

Dr. Celia Miles carefully proofed the manuscript, suggesting ways to improve the flow and maintain the correct points of view.

The Rev. Dwight Christenbury helped with the study questions and offered insightful suggestions on the text itself.

My brother, Patrick (Pete) McLeod, asked questions that led me to simplify some passages.

My husband, Al Lockwood, faithfully read and proofread the many drafts, contributing sage advice and asking probing questions that led to more research, which enriched several passages.

I thank each of these wonderful people for helping me write *The Day After His Crucifixion*.

I also thank you, dear reader, for your interest. You are the reason I wrote this book.

CHAPTER 1

WHAT NOW?

....

I awake with a jerk. Curled tightly on my side, knees drawn up, hands balled into fists near my face, I ache like a wrung-out rag. Cloud filtered light slips through my cottage shutters. Pale, slim rays announcing morning in Jerusalem. My favorite time of day. But I'm exhausted as if it's the middle of the night.

Pushing off the goat-hair covers, I sit up and see that I'm still in yesterday's clothes. And like a lightning flash, the violence rushes back, bending me double from the memory.

Dried blood splatter stains my tunic. His blood.

Yesterday's scenes pierce my heart. The wrathful crowd. Roman soldiers shouting and shoving. Executioners with hammers bending over him, pounding. Blood flying everywhere.

I can't bear the thought that Yeshua has been murdered.

That truth slashes like shattered glass shards. Our Promised One, the man who saved my life, gone. And here I am, breathing. How can this be? It's not right.

On my knees, sobbing, I roll up my sleeping mat with its covers and stash them in the corner. He gave us purpose. He taught us everything. He revealed God as our loving Father. And they've killed him. His healing hands pounded to pulp. His feet viciously impaled. Our strong and gentle master savagely murdered!

I can't stop shivering and I'm not even cold.

Wiping the sleep from my eyes and the tears from my cheeks, I struggle with my jagged thoughts. Will the Romans come for us now? Will those of us following his way be slaughtered next by the Gentile-Romans? What's to become of us?

I shut my eyes and shake my head, doing my best to erase yesterday's savage scenes: his bruised and swollen face. His head encircled by thorns, their spikes tearing his skin. I struggle to slow my sobs, to calm myself, but nothing works. Every breath hurts.

Pouring water from my clay jar into a basin, I wash my face. Repeatedly, I lift my cupped hands of water to my face, but the cool liquid does not soothe. I can't wash away yesterday.

Hate has an odor. It's a stench like old sweat and choking smoke. I smelled it in the crowd with their narrow eyes and hissing voices. It burned my throat and made my eyes water. I smell it still.

Who were those people in the mob and how could they hate him so? How could anyone hate him? His every act was healing. His every word filled with promise: Blessed are the poor, the merciful, the peacemakers. Even his condemnations of hypocrisy were uttered in tearful tones.

Cruelty is normal for the Gentile-Romans. It's to be expected. But I saw Pharisees and Sadducees in the crowd. Temple leaders. City authorities. Their faces smug, even satisfied, their eyes pitiless. What can explain such horror: our leaders approving of the vile Romans torturing one of our own?

Bitterness coats my tongue. I cough and cough, but cannot lose the wretched taste. Yesterday I struggled to stay strong for him, to keep from fainting, to pray without ceasing that the Almighty would send angels to save him.

Over and over I whispered, "Please, Father. Please." Praying for his deliverance. Praying for all we believed in. Praying for him. Praying for us.

And now? Now what?

We who follow him knew that he was God's Promised One. We believed beyond any doubt that he would free us from Rome's evil bonds. He freed so many from sickness and demons, and we who knew his healing touch joyfully supported his ministry. We adored him, were eager for him to restore Israel to greatness. We counted on it.

But now . . . .

I tidy my small table, straighten its covering cloth. With concentration I place the vase and my cutting board and knife in a line just below the table's narrow window. Anything to keep my hands occupied, to try and take my mind off yesterday. Yet the effort fails.

Today is Sabbath. I should go to the temple, but I have no heart for the busy multitudes crowding the courts in celebration of Passover. Just the thought of all those bloody sacrifices, all that burning flesh and the clouds of incense makes me gag.

I sink to the chest beside my table trying to clear my head, to escape the feelings washing over me.

Less than a week ago we accompanied Yeshua on his way to Jerusalem. At the village of Bethphage not far from Bethany, he sent the disciples off to find a young donkey so he could ride into Jerusalem symbolically announcing the coming of God's kingdom. A kingdom of love, grace and compassion. He chose a donkey, the animal of peace, for his procession rather than a horse, the animal of war.

Of course, on the other side of Jerusalem Pilate and his imperial troops were also marching into town, emphasizing the power of our oppressors. Pilate would have to make a show to control the crowds here for Passover. Every year he makes his grand appearance during our sacred festivals. I can almost hear the drumming hoof beats of his horses, can smell the leather armor of his soldiers, can see the long poles topped by sculpted golden eagles. Everything designed to remind us Jews of our proper place in this evil society. Emphasizing who is in charge here.

And there was our precious Yeshua, declaring the message of God's kingdom come, the kingdom of love, peace and compassion.

How my heart thrilled hearing the crowds sing the psalms as he rode: "Blessed is he who comes in the name of the Lord. We bless you from the house of the Lord . . . ."

No weapons of war accompanied Yeshua, just hearts bursting with expectation. The eager crowds sang and spread out palm fronds before him. Some even removed their coats and laid them down for the donkey to walk on. Such loving recognition of our Promised One.

The triumphal words of Zechariah filled me: *"See, your king comes to you, righteous and victorious, lowly and riding on a donkey, on a colt, the foal of a donkey."*

The thrill of hope. At last God's promise was being fulfilled. At long last our King had come.

Where were all those cheering people yesterday? I simply cannot fathom what has happened. Is this how all his healing and teaching will end? My head is a-scramble with questions and fears.

I pour myself a cup of water and sip it slowly. I have no idea of what to do.

Was it only the night before last when we celebrated the Feast of Unleavened Bread together? I helped with meal preparation — the appetizer course with lettuce and dip, the Passover Lamb main course with unleavened bread, the various ceremonial cups. A lovely meal in an equally lovely upper room on Jerusalem's eastern edge. How could we have known it would be our last supper with him?

"Oh, Yeshua, my blessed teacher!" My chest aches so that I can hardly breathe. Jangled thoughts, pain-filled questions tumble together in my throbbing head. Surely I will die right here at my table.

I try to focus on the last supper we shared, treasuring the moments I can recall.

At the table he had seemed pensive, but the disciples were boisterous, sensing something powerful about to happen. I'm sure they expected him to publicly launch his victorious mission as king this week. Certainly everyone in the room expected that. With all the world in town for Passover festivities, this would be his most opportune time.

While we all celebrate God's great deliverance from Egyptian slavery, Yeshua could pronounce his deliverance from Rome. We could barely contain our anticipation. It would happen soon; I could almost taste it.

I caught only some of what was said during dinner as I kept plates coming and cups filled. But I loved the way the candle light set the room aglow making everyone's face rosy.

Near the end of the meal, Yeshua surprised us all by leaving the table and transforming himself into a servant. Removing his outer garment, he wrapped a towel around his waist, filled a basin with water, and then knelt before the disciples one-by-one, and washed their feet.

Lazarus, Martha, Mary, the other servers and I stood in shock, watching from the kitchen doorway. We didn't know what to make of the spectacle.

Peter created quite a fuss, arguing that it was totally inappropriate for a teacher to serve his students in this humble way. But the fuss subsided as Yeshua bantered with him playfully, and (as always) won, saying he was giving us a living example of how we should serve one another. Then he knelt and washed the big fisherman's big feet.

During Yeshua's foot-washing, the other servers and I cleared away the dishes. When I next entered the room, I noticed that Judas had left early. How strange. Yeshua was again seated at the table with the remaining disciples, discussing his future and ours. The room had lost its boisterous energy as the men leaned close to Yeshua, like they couldn't bear to miss a single word from him.

I heard little of what he said, except for this: "A new commandment I give you: Love one another. As I have loved you, so you must love one another. By this all men will know that you are my disciples, if you love one another."

Now those words break my heart.

Then he and the disciples sang a hymn and left for the Mount of Olives. It was already dark.

In the kitchen, as we cleaned the pans and dishes, our hopes rose. Hope that his triumphant moment had come and soon the world would see God's Promised One exalted. Soon we Jews would be freed from our wicked oppressors.

And here I sit, so numb I can't even feel the tears running down my face. I can't stop crying. My gasps and sobs come from a knot in my center that feels like it will squeeze the life out of me.

As the morning light brightens my cottage, I long for sleep or death, anything to blot out yesterday.

Try as I might, I cannot get his feet out of my mind. Swollen blue against the rough upright of the cross, his blood drying in red/ black bubbles. And the huge spikes, furious and demanding.

CHAPTER 2

HE SAVED MY LIFE

....

T he first I ever saw of Yeshua were his feet, the edge of his robe with his dusty toes peeking out from under its fringe. That glimpse seems so long ago now. Another lifetime, another world, even though it has only been three years.

That was the day he saved my life. And much more than that. I remember the long painful path that led me to those blessed feet.

When I was fourteen, my father gave me in marriage to a man older than he was. Even though my father ran a hugely successful business, he was in debt to this man and used me as the payoff.

I'd been suffering strange fits since the age of twelve. I would pass out. Just fall down for no reason and pass out. Mother said foam bubbled from my mouth and my eyes rolled up into my head. She was terrified that I would die. Father was afraid I'd drive him to the poor house. He paid several doctors, but nothing they tried worked, and by the age of fourteen he was sick of dealing with it. He said I was filled with demons and they were ruining his life.

By marrying me off, he got rid of the demon expenses as well as his debt.

Although I did everything my husband asked of me — milled the grain, cooked, cleaned, worked the wool, washed his face and feet when he returned home, even endured the pain of the marriage bed — I could not please him. I bore him no child. So he sold me to another. And my second husband, when he realized I could not give him a son, used me as a weapon to damage a man he believed had wronged him. He cared nothing about my fits, paid no attention to them or me at all, but was seething toward the man he scorned.

Looking back, I see that my husband planned his revenge carefully, cordially inviting his foe to dinner more than once. Insisting that I serve the modest feast wearing clothes he chose for me — close fitting garments of linen that accentuated my seventeen-year-old curves.

After wine and a pleasant meal, the men would talk. I could hear my husband jesting about me. About how the village men all longed for me, his nubile young wife with her beautiful teeth. And the two of them would laugh. But over time, the man my husband hated began to look at me differently, with interest.

It shames me to admit that I welcomed his glances. They were the first such glances I'd ever known. He touched my arm once, just a casual touch, thanking me for refreshing his wine, and that touch stayed with me for days.

I began imagining what life would be like if he were my husband. During feast days, I sought his face among the crowds in the temple courtyard, and if our eyes met, they lingered.

One afternoon when I was alone at home, this man came to the house. Although I told him my husband was not home, he insisted that my husband had told him to drop by. To keep me company for the afternoon. So I prepared a meal for him. I placed bread in a basket, wishing it were fresher. I sliced a leftover chunk of lamb, wishing it were larger. I arranged figs and olives in a bowl for him, wondering why my husband would ask him here when I was alone. But it pleased me to serve him.

When he had eaten his fill and drunk the wine, he pulled me to him. I protested half-heartedly. And when we lay together, I felt for the first time ever, cared for. He held me tenderly, something I'd never known before. He whispered, "So beautiful! So beautiful!" I pulled him close and then, suddenly, my husband burst in with our priest in tow. Shouting in outrage, my husband yanked me up by my hair. Others from the synagogue crowded into the room as I tried to cover myself and slip on my shoes. I only got one shoe on before punishing hands grabbed my tunic and dragged me out to the street.

Neighbors rushed from their homes to see what the ruckus was. I saw mothers trying to shield their toddlers from the frenzied scene. And fathers with faces full of sour disapproval.

I knew my fate: Death. By stoning.

My husband's enemy would be shamed before his family and our whole community. He would not die, but he would be damaged. By catching us together, my husband freed himself of me and wounded the man he hated.

The righteous drove me through the streets, slapping me with their hands and with switches they snapped from nearby trees. They pushed me and yanked my hair hissing like snakes and spitting like camels. I refused to let a sound slip past my lips as I stumbled along, one shoe on one shoe off. I didn't know where I was going, but I knew what the end would be.

And then, in a dusty square just outside the temple walls, they threw me down and kicked me toward a man standing as still and quiet as a statue. My shame kept me on my knees at the man's feet. I stared at the ground and then at the hem of his robe. Beneath the hem's fringe, I glimpsed his toes.

He wore good, solid sandals. His toes looked young and healthy. While the smell of street dust filled my nose, my ears heard the moral indignation of those who had forced me here.

"Teacher, we caught this woman in the very act of adultery," our priest said, with a deep, slow emphasis on "the very act."

Evidently this quiet man was to be my judge and executioner. I dared not move.

"Moses' law demands she die," my husband said, self-righteousness coating every word. "What say you?"

'*Just make it quick*,' I prayed silently.

Instead of speaking, this serene man knelt next to me; his dark eyes catching mine as he leaned forward and with his finger began to write in the dirt. His youth surprised me. He was older than me, of course, but unlike my father and husbands, there were no wrinkles creasing his smooth brow, not one gray hair in his thick, curly beard. And his hands, square and strong, showed no aged veins. He seemed amazingly calm. So calm, I remember thinking he must be in charge of the universe.

I watched his finger write there in the dirt, wondering if he was spelling out how my execution would take place: Who could throw how many stones and what size the rocks could be. '*Make them big. I don't care, just do it quickly.*'

He glanced at me as if he'd heard my prayer. And the words of David's 23rd Psalm suddenly came to me: *"Though I walk through the valley of the shadow of death, I shall fear no evil; for thou art with me; thy rod and thy staff, they comfort me."*

"What say you?" a man's voice insisted. Others grunted, pressing for the verdict. It sounded like a large crowd had gathered, eager to witness the proper punishment due me. On my hands and knees, with my hair hanging shamefully to the dirt, hiding my face, I dared not move.

I felt like a cornered animal. About to be slaughtered.

My judge paused, raised his head, and his eyes swept the men encircling us. "I say, the one who is without sin should cast the first stone." His words wiped the vicious edge off the air. It's almost as if everyone gasped. Then he bent forward and continued writing. The stomping stopped; the questions stopped. I dared not raise my eyes. The only sound I heard was the shuffling of sandals.

After a few moments, my judge stood up and asked, "Where are your accusers?"

I straightened, brushed my hair behind my shoulders and looked around. The square was empty save for my judge and me. My jaw dropped. Not one of those righteous men who'd dragged me here remained. Not even my husband.

"Is there no one to condemn you?" my judge asked, his voice peaceful and untroubled.

I looked up at him and saw such understanding in his face that my heart melted. It was as if he peered into my very soul. As if he actually knew me, knew everything about me and still wanted to protect me. The power of his presence overwhelmed me.

Finally, I whispered, "No, sir."

Reaching down, he took my hand and helped me stand. "Neither do I condemn you. Go, and sin no more."

A gentle silence wrapped itself around me like a cloak. I felt safe. I felt understood and forgiven. It was a feeling of freshness, like a violent storm had passed and in its aftermath, a rainbow shone.

I never returned to my husband's house. And the strange fits never attacked me again.

Yeshua accompanied me to my uncle's home, in Jerusalem's upper city. Uncle Yakov, my mother's oldest brother, never liked my father. He disapproved of father's using me to pay off a debt that he could have easily settled from his own fat wallet. Like my mother and her sisters, Yakov blamed my father for all that had befallen me.

Although he was shocked by my behavior, Uncle Yakov told Yeshua he was grateful I'd now be free of the husband he considered an abomination.

He and Yeshua discussed my future and Uncle Yakov made this cottage a deed of gift to me. At the time, it was the goatherds' abode. Located among the stair streets in the lower city, it served them well and now serves me. Uncle Yakov redesigned it for me. One good-sized room with stout stone walls, a safe door, a window, and a floor of tile. He furnished it for my comfort.

From the top of our street, where the goats have a pasture and a year-round shelter complete with milking room, the Kidron Valley is visible. And up, beyond the Temple Mount, lies the Garden of Gethsemane on the Mount of Olives.

Now I am one of the caretakers of my uncle's goats. I am not allowed around children but I can't corrupt goats. I am well known for the cheese and yogurt I make.

Since the day I met Yeshua, on my knees in the dust, I have never been the same. He breathed the breath of life into that 17-year-old, and for the first time, she became a living soul. Ever since, I have followed him.

My mother and her sisters send me lavish funds, so grateful are they that I no longer am married to a man they all abhorred. With those funds I'm blessed to help Yeshua.

We women who follow the Nazarene keep his purse full. We're grateful to be able to provide for him and the disciples.

From the beginning, his fisherman disciples and we women fervently believed Yeshua would deliver us from Rome. We were certain he is the Promised One who the prophets said would restore God's reign.

Yet we never saw him boast or strut like a warrior. His natural strength was obvious in his well-muscled shoulders and arms. And when he spoke, his words held uncommon authority.

All his teachings focused on God's gracious love and our need to accept that love and share it. His powerful words surely came from beyond this world. His was a force setting us free, rather than pounding us into submission. He healed rather than wounded, forgave rather than condemned. He welcomed the outcast. I am a prime example of that.

We all knew he would rescue us from Rome's vile rule. But they have killed him. How can it be? How can we live without him? And what's to become of us now?

A sudden knock at the door startles me.

CHAPTER 3

THE MORNING AFTER

....

A second rap at the door and, despite my racing heart, I say, "Yes?" The door opens and Sarah ducks inside carrying a small, covered basket.

I must have been too exhausted last night to even bolt my door.

Handing me the basket, she pushes back her mantel. She looks as broken as I feel, bloodshot eyes, face etched with wretchedness. I set the basket on the table, and we embrace, holding each other as our hearts beat and our lungs fill and empty. Burying our faces in each other's shoulders, we let our tunics absorb our tears.

"This is not a day to be alone," she says.

The sound of booted feet marching past outside freezes us both. She whispers, "The soldiers are on patrol everywhere."

We listen for the footfalls to fade. Then, she lifts her basket's covering cloth, revealing grapes, olives, and bread. "Thank you," I whisper.

"Put on something clean," her urges gently. "I'm sure other sisters will be arriving. If ever we've needed one another it's today."

Sarah is old enough to be my grandmother; her wavy white hair shows that. Yet she stands straight as a pillar and is fond of pronouncing she's 'strong as an ox.' Before she met Yeshua, her crippled back bent her nearly double. Like me, her life changed completely because of him.

Following her suggestion, I pull my corner curtain closed, for modesty's sake.

"I'll empty your wash basin," she says and I hear the door open and close.

Reluctantly I remove my blood-spattered tunic, pulling the lamb's wool garment over my head. Somehow, wearing it helped me feel that part of him was still with me. Now, I fold it and lay it on the corner shelf above my bedroll.

"Sarah," I say through my curtain, "Because it's Sabbath, please roll out the rugs."

"Of course, my dear."

It's my Sabbath ritual to unroll the beautiful rugs my mother and aunts gave me when I moved here. To feel the closeness of my mother's loving care on the blessed day of rest comforts me.

I slip into my Sabbath garb: a light blue tunic with dark blue stripes running down to the ankle-length hem. Golden rosettes adorn my sash and its fringe is a brilliant ruby color. I've always loved bright colors, a love no doubt inherited from my mother. She and my aunts are known for the fine fabric they weave and the brilliant colors they use to dye it. My sash is my one indulgence. As I fasten it, I pray a thank you that she and my aunts are safe in Magdala, far from the savage spirit swirling through Jerusalem.

Next, I tend to my hair. It's red and has been the subject of much conjecture. Is it my blessing or my curse? Others seem to know the answer. I only know that it is waist long and takes effort to braid properly. As I comb and weave it, I hear the muffle of other voices, and when I pull back the curtain, my cottage is full of sisters, all with red-rimmed eyes. They have filled my table with baskets of figs, grapes, cheese and bread, and an array of jars and lidded bowls.

Their low, soft voices fill the room with a comforting babble, like a gently flowing brook. As they turn toward me, I feel that we are one — one hurting, throbbing body. I know these women as I know the lines in the palms of my hands.

The sisters of Lazarus. Simon's mother-in-law. As well as Rebekah, Suzanna, Leah, Imma and others. We were all there yesterday. All of us and so many more. Women with their husbands or fathers. Women in pairs. Little knots of women standing together on the edge of the crowd. Or in the middle. So many of us one would have thought the world was made of nothing but weeping women.

Most of the time, we remain invisible within our appointed sphere, out of public view. But yesterday, as word spread of his arrest, rushed trial, and wrongful conviction, we were stunned. We could not believe it. Immediately we headed for Golgotha. Throughout the city we came in twos and threes, rushing, hoping against hope that the rumors were false.

All of Jerusalem, swarming with Passover visitors, was talking about Yeshua the Nazarene. Everyone wanted to see the teacher and healer who challenged the priests and called Israel's One God, "Abba Father" or "Daddy."

The streets were crushed with people and their animals, soldiers and their prisoners, priests and scribes and crowds of Passover visitors. We were bumped and jostled as we made our way, and we had to take care where we stepped because of all the droppings. When Jerusalem swells with feast-pilgrims and their animals, road cleaners cannot keep up.

As we threaded our way through the throngs, we prayed fervently for the rumors to be false.

When we finally made it past the city gates, beyond the tents and campsites of Passover visitors, and started up the dusty path toward Golgotha, I could see that the soldiers already had two men hanging from crosses, their long hair floating on the mid-morning breeze. Neither man was Yeshua. But the soldiers were bending over a third cross, laying on the ground.

As the sun's rays warmed our path, puffs of dust rose like little brown clouds at our feet. We pushed our way up the hill, straining to see who the third man was. "Please not Yeshua. Please! Please!" I prayed.

But at the top of the arid skull-like hill, we saw. There on the third cross, his bruised and bleeding body was bound in place by ropes as the soldiers nailed him to the wood. His eyes were swollen nearly shut in his discolored face, a crown of thorns ringed his beautiful head, and blood flowed from his mouth and nose.

"Oh, what have you done to him!" I turned away, unable to look. Other women's voices wailed. I wanted to run away, but I could not leave him. Instead, I stuffed the end of my head mantle into my mouth to stifle my sobs and eased as close as I could to him.

I simply couldn't believe what was happening. Our cherished Promised One, the man whose loving care had healed so many, the man who proclaimed the coming of God's kingdom, whose whole life emphasized compassion and healing, was being crucified. And surrounding the scene, a restless crowd clamored for his death.

I heard him say, "Father forgive them for they know not what they do." His precious voice, cracked with pain, the voice that had said "neither do I condemn you" asking forgiveness for his executioners. Even they, with their bloody hammers, were recipients of his love. Yet they knew nothing of this gift as they focused on their brutal task.

We watched while the soldiers nailed a walnut placard above his head. Cross placards, painted white, with red lettering, announce the crime for which the criminal is being executed. What could Yeshua's crime be? A man near me read the words aloud: "Yeshua the Nazarene, King of the Jews." Leaning in, I could see that that statement was written in three languages: Hebrew, Greek and Latin.

Obviously, the Gentile-Romans wanted all the world to know they were executing our Promised One.

So they're killing him as a political rebel? "Please, Oh Holy One," I begged. "Save him. You sent him here for us. I'm certain of that. Please save him!"

As the soldiers finished nailing the placard and were preparing to raise the cross with its human burden, temple officials rushed up and began loudly protesting. The soldiers with hammers just stood there listening, their arms hanging by their sides. My hopes soared. Maybe the priests would save Yeshua.

But, I realized that the priests weren't trying to save him. They were arguing over the wording on the placard, and despite their passion, their waving arms and raised voices, the soldiers pushed them back.

Then the soldiers, leaning together, slid the foot of the cross into its hole, and raised it upright. They wedged rocks large and small in around it to hold it securely in its standing position between the other two crosses. Yeshua hung there, blood dripping from his hands.

Vomit filled my mouth with sour mush. I spit it out and held onto the woman next to me to keep from fainting. Women from throughout the gathering crowd wailed and beat their breasts.

Men in the mob shouted insults as Yeshua struggled to breathe. Where did such cruelty come from? They seemed a scowling crowd of demons. Although I dared not glare at those who mocked Yeshua, if I could have, I would have destroyed them instantly. But I was helpless. We all were.

As the morning wore on, the sounds of women weeping continued to fill the air. My shock gave way to wretchedness and grief.

At one point, I saw him speak with one of the other men being crucified, but I couldn't make out the words. He never answered any of the taunts from the mob.

One by one the disciples slipped away. No doubt they were as frightened as we were. Merciless Rome is famous for cruelty. Everyone knows that. Those in power love bloody scenes. They love to bully and torture. They're experts at it.

Yet, despite our fears, most of the other women and I stayed, standing as close as we dared, praying and weeping. After all he had done for me, I couldn't leave him to suffer alone.

At this time of year it can be cold one day, hot the next. This morning's chill disappeared and by mid-day the sun's heat sent sweat streaming down our necks and backs.

"How could the Almighty allow this execution?" The question hovered among us like a whining mosquito.

Our backs ached. Our knees ached. The muscles of our necks quivered from our upward gazing. But our physical discomfort was nothing. Nothing compared to our shattered souls. Nothing compared to his torture.

In the late afternoon, a mysterious blackness, silent and heavy as wet wool, settled over Golgotha like a mushroom cap and hid Yeshua's suffering. It felt empty and coolly frightening, like everything else about this day. It blotted out any glimmer of light, hiding us even from one another. Yet we women stayed, wrapped in our confusion and grief.

At the ninth hour as the Passover lambs were being slain at the temple, when the priests held their basins of gold and silver under each lamb's neck to catch the blood, while the Levites chanted the Hallel Psalms so loudly that we could actually hear their voices rising above the city's din, at that very moment, Yeshua declared, "It is finished." And the blackness faded as quickly as it had come. His powerful, authoritative words were not those of a defeated, dying man. But then I saw his head drop and his chest grow still. And my heart broke.

We women witnessed it all. Beginning to end. The execution of the most perfect person to ever walk our earth.

Now grieving sisters fill my cottage. Some sit on the floor, some stand, leaning against the wall; the two oldest sit on my tableside chest, each holding a basket of food on her lap.

"Welcome, my sisters," I say. "And as Yeshua would say, Peace be with you." My heart swells with love for these dear women. Hopefully they can feel it. "And thank you for filling my home with your presence. I don't think I could bear being alone today." My voice breaks. I brush away my tears. A compassionate murmur pervades the room. Sarah slips her arm around me.

Everyone is dressed in Sabbath clothes, filling the room with color and beauty. We should be in sackcloth and ashes, which would more accurately express my bitter grief.

Nonetheless, I'm grateful at this moment to simply be with these sisters who, like me, have followed, listened to and learned from our beloved teacher. Like me, they have known his healing touch. Like me, they have heard his stories, treasured his instructions, pondered his example. And, like me, they were there yesterday, faithful to the end.

After many tearful embraces, I move to the far side of my table and rest against the wall next to my window, wishing I could think of more to say, but I am empty.

Someone begins the mourning song and one by one the rest of us join in, our sad and earnest voices rising like a plume of incense.

> "Consider, and call for the mourning women to come;
> send for the skillful women to come;
> let them make haste and raise a wailing over us,
> that our eyes may run down with tears, and our eyelids gush with water.
> For a sound of wailing is heard from Zion:
> How we are ruined!"

We sing the familiar words over and over like a chant, like the wind moaning through winter's barren trees. We breathe the words, sigh the words, pray the words. And when we finally sing ourselves out, we are silent. Together.

Sarah is the first to speak. "Who is caring for his mother?"

"John took her to his home."

"Ahhhh, yes."

I recall Yeshua's instructions when despite his shuddering pain, he spoke to John, transferring his mother's care to his young disciple. What must today be like for her? How can she endure it?

Sarah sighs and says, "It was a Sabbath when he freed me. A Sabbath like today. Well, not exactly like today. But a Sabbath with sunshine and birdsong.

"I was bent double. You may remember me from those days. My knees hurt. My ankles hurt. My back, oh how it hurt. I spent eighteen years in that painful position. Eighteen years bent over, always staring at the ground. I had to use a walking stick to keep my balance. Just try shopping at the market when you're bent double and holding onto a walking stick.

"And when I awoke that Sabbath morning, I had no expectation of that day being any different for me. I crawled out of bed and struggled to dress, my back hurting as usual, all my joints snapping and popping as I put on my sandals and left for the temple.

"When you're bent and crippled as I was, no one looks at you or speaks to you. Or if they do, it's always with sadness in their voice. Anyone who ever paid attention to me was sad.

"But on that Sabbath morning, as I shuffled along in my pain and loneliness, He called out to me. From across the temple courtyard, this cheerful, friendly voice, almost like a hand reaching out to me. 'Woman,' he called. 'You are freed from your infirmity.'

"Those were his exact words. 'You are freed.'

"I heard those words as clear as can be despite the din. You know how it is in the courtyard with the livestock and the teachers and the food stalls and water sellers, and in spite of all that racket, I heard this friendly voice say, 'woman, you are freed.'"

She shakes her head, fresh amazement filling her features. "I heard those words and didn't know what they meant. Was he calling to me? Why? What was I freed from? I'd never asked to be freed. I looked at that handsome young man, full to the brim with life. You could see the enthusiasm shining from his eyes and his smile. It was like he had a wonderful surprise for me. And I didn't know what to think. I stopped shuffling and stood still wondering why in the world this young man would be calling out to me. And he headed my way, full of eagerness. He reminded me of one of my grandsons when they were little, running to show me something they'd discovered like a bug or a rock. He came right to me, took my elbow and I stood up straight."

She laughs at the memory and we all laugh with her. In the midst of our grief we feel her joy and it rises like bubbles within us.

"I was so surprised," she says. "For the first time in all those long, painful years, I stood up straight. Just like that! Ah! It felt good! I could look around from an upright position. I'm telling you, there was no pain, none whatsoever. And it's been that way ever since.

"He seemed as delighted as I was.

"Oh, there was quite a commotion with the local priest. He thought healing was work and it should never take place on the Sabbath. Especially in *his* synagogue. He made some outlandish remarks and people began clucking their tongues.

"But, Yeshua reminded the priest that everyone frees their ox or ass from their stalls on the Sabbath and leads them to water so they can drink. And then he said the most amazing thing." she pauses for a moment. "He said, 'Should not this woman, a daughter of Abraham whom Satan has bound for eighteen years, be loosed from the bond on the Sabbath day?' And all the tongue clicking stopped and people actually began applauding.

"He called me 'a daughter of Abraham.' Have you ever heard that designation before? It felt like . . . I don't know, like being publicly welcomed into the family. Being called a daughter of Abraham was the finishing touch on his marvelous gift to me. A gift I never even asked for.

"I praised God that with a word and a touch this amazing young man set me free. I praise God today for him!" Her voice begins to break. "I don't understand how the Almighty, blessed be He, could allow them to do what they did to him yesterday." Her face collapses into her hands. Her whole body shakes as she weeps. We wipe our eyes. With a large, wavering sigh, she adds, "but I am going to continue praising him for the rest of my life. To me, this old woman, he shall always be full of life and healing. I am a living testament to his power."

And Sarah begins to hum. Others pick up her melody. For several minutes my cottage is filled with gentle humming. The melody makes me feel less broken.

Then Simon's mother-in-law speaks. "I also praise him," she says. "As you know, he banished my fever by simply touching my hand." She lifts her right hand as though looking at it for the first time. "I was really sick, burning up with fever. But, unlike my sister Sarah here, my fever would pass. It was not life threatening, nothing as dramatic as her eighteen years of suffering.

"It's abundantly clear to me that Yeshua did not want people to be sick. He did not want people to suffer. He came in the door with my son and the others. They were all laughing and talking, and he walked straight over to where I was lying and took this hand and like that, just like that, I was well. The fever left me and I felt whole and energetic. In fact, I felt better than I had in years."

The sisters murmur, sharing stories of their own, commenting on others' tales. We've heard many of these stories before. Even the men have repeated them. But today it's clear we need to share them amongst ourselves. We must keep them alive.

Yeshua filled our hearts with hope, something we hadn't had as a people in generations. And late yesterday, as Sabbath drew near, I watched his lifeless body being taken down from the cross. I simply cannot believe that he is gone. How can such a big, powerful, loving life be snuffed out like that?

It tears at my soul to hear us speak of him in the past tense. How could The Almighty allow such an atrocity?

Turning to the table of food, I begin to fill serving baskets with olives, cheese, figs, grapes and bread. It's a relief to have something useful to do, something I can concentrate on so that I don't keep tumbling helplessly through yesterday's horrors.

"Let me help," Lazarus' sister Martha whispers as she comes up beside me. I hand her baskets, and she places them about on the carpets so everyone can easily reach and partake of the contents. There is comfort in sharing a meal, isn't there. We have shared so many, though none as sad as today's.

Then, Martha takes my water jug and a towel, and I take my small basin. We move from sister to sister as each one briefly rinses her hands in preparation of eating. Finished with hand-washing, I pray a blessing and pass the wineskin and we begin our impromptu meal.

From the way everyone scoops up the fruit and bread it's obvious that we're all famished. I don't think I ate anything yesterday. I didn't think I'd be able to eat today, but everything tastes wonderful! I love the happy little sounds people make when they enjoy what they're eating. Those gentle, grateful sighs now fill my cottage. As I push open the window lattice, the room brightens, its whitewashed plaster walls reflecting the spring sun's glow.

"We've got to do something," Imma says, pounding the floor beside her, apparently strengthened by our meal. "We can't just let this brutal murder go unnoticed."

What can we do, I wonder. I look at my hands laying helpless in my lap. Then I find myself staring at Imma's shorn head as she and others discuss the need to do something about yesterday's execution. Like many women dismissed to the streets by husbands who no longer want them, she had worked as a prostitute, earning barely enough to stay alive. It's a miserable choice for women with no family wealth to rely on and no male relative to support them. They can beg. Or they can sell what they have. Such painful choices in a society full of priests and elders preaching purity and piousness.

No wonder Yeshua condemned dismissal and divorce, calling the practice of men hard-hearted. No wonder Imma and others like her have found such comfort in following Yeshua. Unfortunately, she hasn't been able to escape street violence. Recently, a former customer beat her and shaved her head to humiliate her.

But, and I find this admirable, she accepts no humiliation. Today, she sits nearly bald, full of dignity and confidence. Although her life has changed dramatically because of Yeshua, what fascinates me at this moment is the new hair she is sprouting. It's coming in curly and black and I'm wondering if her skull shivers from the cold. And then I'm ashamed of my shallowness. Our world has been destroyed by the vicious Gentile-Romans and I'm musing about what it feels like to have no hair. What is wrong with me!

"There must be something we can do," Imma insists. "We should go to the priests and demand they raise a clamor with the governor."

Rebekah, seated near the door, laughs bitterly. "The priests? They're in it up to their haughty noses. They've been after him since the first time he made that big scene in the temple, throwing out the money changers and saying they'd turned God's house into a den of thieves. Didn't you see them at Golgotha?"

Her words echo my own broken hearted questions.

"We must not question The Almighty," someone says. "At least He hid Yeshua's suffering. How can the priests explain yesterday's blackness?"

Another woman quickly adds, "And I heard that the temple curtain between the holy and most holy places ripped from top to bottom. Now the most holy place is wide open, totally exposed.

"What's that all about?" someone asks.

Precisely my question. Is the torn curtain story true? Is the most holy place, where The Almighty has actually met with priests now open to all eyes? And if so, what does it mean?

"It's a signal," an unfamiliar voice says, as if speaking to herself. We turn to a frail woman in the corner. She seems surprised that we have heard her. "Well," she says. "Consider this. If it was rent from top to bottom it had to be torn by an angel or perhaps The Almighty himself. No human could accomplish that. And none of the priests would do such a thing. So, I think it's a signal or symbol, a message."

Imma asks, "Of what?"

The frail woman is silent for a long moment. "Perhaps it signals that the Almighty, blessed be He, will no longer limit himself to a small space in a temple that human hands have built."

Imma says, "Or that he's sick of the priests' corruption and will no longer reside there."

Other voices offer other explanations. The stories, the rumors, the questions continue. My cottage is a-chatter, yet we keep our voices low. We must not draw attention to our gathering.

Everyone has something to say. Outrage fills us. Outrage and grief and emptiness and fear. But we have no answers. We want so badly to do something about Yeshua's grotesque crucifixion. But what can we do?

After all our protestations, all our angry proclamations, we know we are helpless and an anguished silence settles in. Yeshua is dead, and we're adrift in a darkly dangerous world with no way out.

CHAPTER 4

MOURNING TOGETHER

The day progresses. My cottage door opens often admitting sisters I recognize and sisters I've never seen before, until the room feels like it will burst. Some carry suckling infants, some bring baskets of food, others bring reed pipes that they play, adding mournful music to our grief-filled gathering. Here we are, all of us longing for companionship on this Passover Sabbath.

When Joanna arrives, I'm both surprised and pleased. She is the wife of King Herod's steward, Chuza, and she was with us yesterday, watching as two men well along in years placed Yeshua's precious body in the tomb.

As Chuza's wife, Joanna is a woman of high rank, well aware of the currents of intrigue swirling around King Herod's throne. Yet she has never hidden her dedication to Yeshua. And she never wavered at yesterday's crucifixion.

She enters wearing a fine tunic and head mantle. The embroidery is as intricate and colorful as that of Uncle Yakov's cloaks. While many despise her for her close connection to Herod, pagan idolater that he is, we women who love Yeshua love her too. She has been faithful and generous to his cause.

And yesterday, at the cross, I saw her strength. She remained all day, a witness to the Roman's savagery. Even after he bowed his head and died, she stayed.

Most of the mocking mob had wandered away during the darkness. But Joanna and the rest of us women stayed, praying, weeping, wondering what would become of our teacher's body. It would have been proper for the disciples to claim it, but they were out of sight. Understandably so.

As the sun slunk westward and long shadows crept toward Jerusalem, we saw the men: two older men carrying burial cloths. I recognized one as Joseph of Arimathea, a prominent member of the Sanhedrin, our Jews' supreme council.

About the same time, a Roman soldier arrived with a heavy pipe and spear. He went to each of the others being crucified and with the pipe broke their legs. Their moaning filled the air. When he came to Yeshua, he felt his legs, then looked long at the limp body. With his spear he pierced Yeshua's side and water and blood burst out .

The officer lowered his head and said sadly, "Surely this was the Son of God." Joanna, the other women, and I exchanged glances. Why couldn't that soldier have recognized our Promised One earlier and saved him?

Joseph handed him an official looking document. After reading it, the soldier said, "Wait here until I return." Then he hurried back down the hill.

We wondered what now?

Joseph obviously had enough public standing to convince Pilate, the governor of our area, to let him have Yeshua's body. But who was the other older man? These two were surely risking their reputations, if not their lives.

Eventually, the soldier returned with three younger men each carrying a ladder and long rope. The soldier had a body pallet which he laid on the ground and told Joseph to prepare it for Yeshua's body.

Leaning their ladders against three sides of the cross, the younger men climbed and went to work. With the ropes, they secured Yeshua's body to the cross. Joanna and I winced and wept as they straightened, then pulled out the blood covered spikes. First, feet. One youth supported his body while the other two removed the nails from his swollen hands. Then they loosened the ropes and together slowly lowered Yeshua's lifeless form onto the linen burial cloth the older men had spread out. Their job done, they took their ladders and ropes and left.

Now the older men went to work. They gently drew Yeshua's outstretched arms together and tenderly bound them at the wrists with linen strips so that his body could be properly wrapped. Each man kissed his bloodied hands. Precious hands that had dispensed blessings and healings, that had held little children and healed the sick.

The men repeatedly wiped their eyes while they worked.

With great care they removed the wicked, thorny crown, easing it from Yeshua's hair and forehead. Once free, Joseph angrily flung it away. Then, like a loving father, he smoothed Yeshua's hair into place.

Next they wrapped his head and body. When they bent over, hands on knees, breathing heavily from their efforts, I feared they would not have the strength to finish their task before sunset, the coming of the Sabbath.

Their wrapping finally complete, Joseph, the other older man, and the soldier carried the pallet with Yeshua's enshrouded body down the hill. We women followed.

Three men with a body and a band of weeping women walked slowly down Golgotha's dusty path, then around the bottom of the hill to the cemetery where they laid him in a new limestone tomb.

I praise Joseph and the other man for claiming our Promised One's body. If they had not taken charge, Yeshua would likely have been tossed in the ravine as criminals are to become food for jackals and other wild animals.

Joanna also risked the reputations of her husband and herself by attending the crucifixion and staying with the rest of us women to watch the burial. Yet, she showed no such concern. If any among us characterize Yeshua's teaching that the greatest must become a servant, it has been Joanna. She has given liberally to the Master's cause, has served in every capacity required and stayed through all of yesterday's horrors.

Today she comes in the door bringing fig cakes and honey comb. "They say honeycomb is the food of angels," she whispers, a little smile flitting across her face. "If we ever needed such food it's today."

Now, as the sisters talk and share, weeping one moment, then chuckling the next, Joanna joins Martha and me at the table where we're organizing the leftovers from our morning meal.

"The second man we watched bury Yeshua yesterday is Nicodemus," she tells me. "My husband says he's a prominent Pharisee."

"So Yeshua has devotees in both the Sanhedrin and among the Pharisees," I say. "You would think they might have tried to stop his execution." My words emerge bitter and sharp.

She raises her eyebrows, "They may have tried for all we know," she whispers. "Claiming and burying his body took amazing courage. And love."

I thought by now I'd be all cried out, but my tears rise anew at her words.

Salome's voice fills my cottage. She recites a poem her mother taught her, a poem that is supposed to calm and comfort us. And all the while, I'm wondering why no one with authority — religious or governmental — stopped Yeshua's crucifixion.

When Salome finishes, Sarah and Imma urge Leah to tell her experience. Leah's story has given me shivers every time I've heard it.

Leah was once a wealthy woman. Her silver hair, falling in waves over her shoulders, and her soft, round face, give no hint of the trials she has endured. Her voice is serene as the Pool of Bethesda at sunrise. No indication of all she's lost.

"As you well know," she begins. Other voices still and we turn to her, "I suffered for years from bleeding. It began some time after the birth of my last baby… just a few drops." She smoothes the ripples of her skirt. "But as time passed and the drops continued, I became concerned. Our family physician encouraged me to drink a certain potion. It was expensive and difficult to make, but I drank it for months.

It was so bitter, it did nothing but spoil my appetite. And my mood." Gentle laughter rises among us.

"Not only did the medicine fail to help, in truth my problem increased until I had a continual, light flow.

"As you can imagine, this caused great contention in our household. Being perpetually unclean did not contribute to a satisfying marriage." There are sympathetic nods all around.

"Nonetheless, my good husband was patient. He took me to many physicians and spent a fortune on specialists, but my problem intensified. I grew pale and weak and suffered constantly from exhaustion. Some days I didn't even have enough energy to leave my bed. After several years it became clear that whatever the cause, my condition was incurable."

She sighs. And there are echoing sighs throughout the room. We know the outcome. Her patient husband died. She lost her family due to her condition and she became like a leper — unclean and outcast.

"That was my life for years," she shakes her head sadly, remembering her pain-filled loneliness. "Then I heard about Yeshua the Nazarene and his gift of healing. And not just for men. I heard about Sarah. Eighteen years changed with a word and a touch. I heard about children healed, and the blind man at the Pool of Siloam who received his sight, and many other healings. And you know what really struck me?"

Imma says, "That he didn't charge a fee." Everyone laughs including Leah.

"Well, after all my doctors, that was certainly a big surprise," Leah says with a smile. "But what really struck me was that the majority of people receiving his blessing of good health were not among the privileged. Most of those he healed were like me, unimportant nobodies. And that, my dear sisters, that gave me hope. I determined to find him and beg for healing. For twelve miserable years I had tried everything and I had lost everything. This teacher from Nazareth was my only hope. I felt certain he could cure me."

She pauses. We all wait. We know her story, but we long to hear it fresh from her lips. Stories come alive in the telling and in the hearing. And today we are desperate to bring our stories about him to life. To keep Yeshua's spirit among us. She gazes around the room, at all the lovely sisters waiting for her to continue.

"I heard that he and his disciples were in Capernaum for a few days, so I went there. It was easy to find him. He was in the center of a big crowd just outside the synagogue. I could see him talking to the local rabbi, listening intently to the rabbi, and nodding his head.

"I wrapped my tunic and mantle tightly around myself and began squeezing through the crowd to get as close to him as possible. It wasn't easy, let me tell you. But I was determined. And then the crowd, like one large being, began to move. From the comments of those near me I learned that the rabbi's twelve-year old daughter had died and Yeshua was going to his home to bring the girl back to life.

"We'd all heard about Lazarus, so there was no doubt what would happen. My problem seemed so shallow compared to the death of a child. After all, I'm an old woman. My life is all behind me, why should I bother him with my request? Still, I hurried as fast as I could and squeezed through and soon I was beside him, matching him stride for stride. This close." She holds up her thumb and forefinger to show that she was right next to him.

"I could see a line of sweat running down beside his ear, disappearing into his beard. I was amazed at his beautiful, unruly eyebrows shading those large, dark eyes.

"I stepped back a little, thinking it was too presumptuous to stop him in his mission. Then the idea came to me … I didn't have to speak to him. I didn't have to stop him on his way. If I could simply touch the hem of his garment… that's all it would take and I'd be healed."

We all know how forbidden it is for a woman to touch a man without his permission. But worse, an *unclean* woman touching a man without his permission, well … brazen doesn't come close to describing the act.

"I know," she holds up her hands, palms out. "I know it was wrong. Yes, it violated every religious rule and social code…but, sisters, I was desperate. I hadn't been able to see my grown children in years. And I had grandchildren I could not even touch. Can you imagine!" She closes her eyes. "Still, I didn't want to interrupt him on his way to the little girl."

She wipes tear paths from her cheeks. And wipes them again. Then clears her throat.

"The crowd was pushing and jostling, everyone wanting to be as close to him as possible, and I, I leaned over and just gently ran my fingers through the fringe on the hem of his robe. It wasn't more than a moment's contact, the soft silky fringe flowing across my fingers, and just like that, my bleeding stopped. I stood still from the most incredible sensation I'd felt in twelve years — the feeling of no sensation, no flow. I felt healthy and strong and energetic and happy! The crowd pressed past me. I took a deep breath and uttered a silent prayer of gratitude.

"Then," she raises her eyebrows and pauses for suspense. "Everything and everyone came to a complete standstill. And he said, 'Who touched me?' He looked around. When his eyes met mine, I knew he knew and I saw no condemnation. None at all.

"Oh, his disciples were saying, 'Everyone's touching you, Teacher. Look at the crowd. You can't help but be touched.' They had no idea."

We all chuckle. We know the disciples. We love them, we do, but they often have no idea of what's going on. And they are so competitive, always striving to be number one with him. The position of first is very important to them. Certainly they didn't want him to stop. They wanted him to get to the rabbi's house immediately and perform his mighty act immediately. Then they could stand beside him as the accolades rained down.

"But he did not budge," Leah continues. "His gaze was fixed on me and I properly lowered my eyes." Her voice breaks and she takes a moment to compose herself. "I bowed to the earth and said, I touched you, Sir. In my heart, I said, Thank you, my lord. You have restored my life. And I will never forget his words to me. They were like healing waters to my soul. He said, 'Daughter, *your* faith has made you whole.'"

I shake my head at her story and wipe my eyes. No word of reproof for her abominable behavior. No shrinking back from her uncleanness. Not a word of condemnation. Not a word of correction. Not a word of instruction. To credit her for her faith in so public a way is unheard of! Yet it is so like him, isn't it.

Leah is weeping heavily now, but after a moment regains her composure. "And I have never been the same. He called me 'daughter' as if he were my kinsman. As if he were restoring my family as well as my health. He delivered me and gave me life — a new life. And, like Sarah, I shall praise him until they lay me in my grave."

Murmurs of "Yes, yes." fill my cottage.

That we can do: we can praise him for he surely deserves our praise. We can share our stories of what he has done for us.

"And lest I forget," Lea says, "Yeshua went on to the rabbi's house and raised the child from her deathbed. On that day he gave new life to this old woman and that twelve-year-old girl."

Lazarus's sisters begin to sing. Their voices are so lovely. Mary's pure, clear soprano and Martha's gentle, rich alto blend in perfect harmony. One by one, we all join in, singing praises to the Almighty.

I can't believe I'm praising God. How can I sing praises when the one who did so much good, who showed and taught compassion, who proclaimed the coming of God's kingdom is dead? But the singing soothes me. Our voices, blending in tenderness and longing, rise like prayer.

After our song, other women, my sisters in grief, share memories of how Yeshua changed them.

A woman I do not recognize stands. "I need to stretch out after sitting for so long," she explains as she leans against the wall. She makes me think of a lanky youth, yet she's older than a youth.

"I am grateful for your stories," she says. "They help complete my understanding of Yeshua and his teachings. I must admit I have followed him from afar. My husband and I have six children. Three boys. Three girls. They keep us too busy for our own good, but we have found time to listen to Yeshua when he's teaching in the synagogue.

"And sometimes we have seen him in the street, with his disciples. I've heard his hearty laughter and watched him gather up the kiddies in his big embrace. But until I heard him describe the Kingdom of God, and reveal that kingdom through his words and actions, I lived in fear.

"How could God love me, a sinner? I lose my temper with the kids. I get angry at my husband. My mother-in-law and I often butt heads. No matter how hard I try, I sin and I've been taught that God abhors sinners. So, I've lived in fear of The Almighty, knowing he abhors me.

"But when I heard Yeshua's story of the father welcoming back his prodigal son, a light went on in my heart. I suddenly understood why he calls The Almighty 'Father' or 'Daddy.' The God he revealed, the God he showed us and encouraged us to love is not filled with wrath at our failures. He is waiting with a love-filled heart to gather us in, welcome us home.

"Yeshua's teaching replaced my fear with love and gratefulness. I understand The Almighty in a whole different way now because of him. And it has changed my life completely."

She moves toward the door. With her hand on the latch, she adds. "That is my miracle story. How he took away my fear and filled me with love." Then she thanks me and heads out. Two others join her as she leaves.

I stand near my table, watching the sad and beautiful faces in my house, feeling the afternoon breeze flow in through the window, listening to the rustle of bare branches in the afternoon wind. How was it that Yeshua raised the little girl and raised Lazarus after the man was four-days dead, and yet that life-giving power eluded him yesterday?

Glancing at Martha, who is standing nearby, I motion her over. She bends low to hear what I have to say.

"Don't you wonder why he didn't save himself?" I feel almost like my question, my doubts, my fears are all sins that need forgiving. But the Promised One who could explain is gone. And I am left with nothing but sorrow.

Our eyes meet and she nods, her lips form a straight, loose line. "How do you explain it?" I whisper.

She simply shakes her head.

Imma's voice rises, "I'm embarrassed to say this, but I'm not only destroyed by yesterday's murder by the cursed Gentile-Romans, I'm also angry. I'm angry at The Almighty, blessed be He. And I think I'm angry at Yeshua."

Her words snap our heads around like a slap in the face. "What?" comes from several sisters.

Imma continues, her voice trembling, "I'm heartbroken. But surely he had the power to prevent his crucifixion. Surely! He saved us all and would not save himself."

Martha says, "You sound like one of yesterday's mob."

"Am I the only one who feels this way?" she looks around the room. No one meets her eyes. "Or am I the only honest one here?" her voice breaks but she keeps talking. "I'm so heartbroken I could die. How could this crucifixion take place? Oh I understand the politics of it all right. Clear as can be." She's sobbing now, coughing and sobbing, but still talking. "But no one saved him. Not even he himself. He was our Promised One, our Messiah come to deliver us from Roman rule, and Roman rule killed him. He's dead. Gone. Why? Why? Why?"

Joanna raises her hand, motioning for silence. "There may have been men who tried to save him. The Marys and I watched two older men take his body to a newly excavated stone tomb just before the start of Sabbath last evening. One of those men is Joseph of Arimetha, a prominent member of the Sanhedrin. Who knows what he might have said to try and change yesterday's verdict? My husband Chuza told me Joseph was not among the Sanhedrin officials who brought Yeshua up on charges before Pilate and then Herod.

64

"The other man we saw last evening is a prominent Pharisee, Nicodemus. Surely these two well-established, highly respected men have risked all to save our precious Yeshua's body. And surely they represent others who care. We are not alone in our sorrow and loss.

"And Chuza told me something else, too. He said that both Pilate and Herod gave Yeshua an opportunity to defend himself and our blessed teacher remained silent. Silent as a lamb being led to the slaughter."

Gasps fill the room. Eyes flash from one to another. Shock permeates the air. Who can explain his refusal to defend himself, his refusal to be saved? Martha's sister, Mary, who has been sitting demurely, clears her throat. All eyes turn toward her.

"Yeshua was my brother Lazarus' best friend. He spent many days and nights at our home. As you are all well aware, Yeshua restored life to my brother four days after he succumbed to a deadly fever. I love Yeshua with all my heart and, like you, I believe his teaching and choose to follow his way. But today I am trying to draw hope or peace from the fact that Yeshua's every word and every act had a purpose. I would even go so far as to say a divine purpose. Of all the men I have ever seen, the priests, the scribes, the teachers, even men in my family, Yeshua seemed like God on earth to me. Surely you recognize the truth of my words.

"He taught us how to be human. He showed us the way of life centered on God's kingdom of forgiveness and compassion.

"Like all of you, my sisters in his service, I am broken. No explanation for yesterday can comfort me. But despite our despair, and even our anger, I must believe that something good will come of this."

Immediately our long-repressed wailing erupts, misery and sorrow pouring forth until my cottage vibrates with the sounds of agony. Mary's words, spoken with such loving assurance, have pierced our anguished hearts and our grief can no longer be restrained.

When two of the infants raise their voices, their mothers quickly take their leave. Inside, voices rise and fall, howl and moan, wail and bawl and groan and shriek until I'm sure we will all cry ourselves blind. How I wish something good would come of yesterday's horror. But I see nothing in the atrocity to offer hope. Not even a flicker.

A powerful pounding on my door stuns us all to silence. The sisters quickly muffle their sobbing, and bend double, hiding their tear-washed faces in their skirts. Certain that the Romans have come to haul us off, I nervously pull on a mantle and step outside.

CHAPTER 5

SURPRISE AT THE GOAT PASTURE

....

For the second time today, icy fear has chilled my wounded heart, only to be suddenly, completely relieved. No soldier stands armed and angry at my door. Instead, Uncle Yakov in his finest Sabbath tunic and ruby red cloak greets me with a face full of concern.

"At Temple this morning I heard about your teacher," he says. I lower my eyes, bow my head and struggle to maintain my composure. "I am sorry, my child. Truly sorry."

My tears gush and I'm unable to speak for their flow. His arms surround me, pulling me to his ample chest. His embrace feels like a blessing.

"What's going to happen to us now?" I whisper.

"Who can say, my child? Only YHWH."

And where was YHWH yesterday? I think, blackness pooling in my heart.

Uncle Yakov holds me at arms length. "What is all the wailing coming from your house?"

"The sisters. They've gathered here."

"Well, I'll give you this advice. Shhhhhh! This is no time to draw attention to yourselves. The entire city is on edge."

I nod.

"Soldiers are everywhere," he says.

"I know. I know." I sob silently into his tunic, his arms around me once again. "Why did this happen? He didn't preach rebellion, only peace."

After a moment, Uncle Yakov says, "His message was not received that way by those in charge. And you know the Roman pleasure in violence."

He places a fat little packet in my hand. "You may need this. Now go back to your guests. And, please," he presses his finger to my lips, "keep them quiet."

Glancing into the packet, I find it filled with gold coins. When I look up to thank him, I see his back halfway up the street, his bright cloak swaying as he heads for his home in the upper city.

Slipping the packet into my pocket, I step back inside and urge quietness. Someone is playing the reeds, a low, sad, funeral dirge. The music moves among us all like a muddy flow, dark and heavy. We're exhausted. Two of the women close their eyes as if in prayer, only to nod off. Others whisper together.

I try to clear my tangled emotions. Would that I had died yesterday instead of Yeshua. But here I am, full of sorrow and memories and scenes and confusion. Full and empty at the same time.

Was the dinner in Bethany only a week ago? It takes my breath away to think how recently we were celebrating together. And now here we are, all together grieving. It is more than I can handle; I need to clear my head.

"I have to water the goats," I say softly, in case anyone is listening, and grabbing my clay water jar, step outside.

A quiet coolness fills the street. It is, after all, the Sabbath. Even though it's early spring with the barley already ripe and birdsong in the air, I can tell there will be rain. I can smell it. A little leftover winter rain. The latter rain the farmers all count on. Rain suits my misery.

It feels good to move, although I move in a fog. My head is a jumble. It's an effort to breathe. How can the sun shine, the wind blow, the clouds amble across the sky? How can it be such a beautiful afternoon when he is dead?

I climb the street steps to the field where the goats graze. The animals with their intense, weird eyes stop eating or head butting and stare at me expectantly. They know I've come to give them something. As I open the gate and step inside, they gather round, nudging one another and me and making their friendly little sounds. They have no idea of the tragedy that has taken place.

"Yes, yes, I've come to give you a drink," I say, and lower the well jug. When I pour the water into their trough, they stretch out their necks and start drinking, their little tails standing straight up and quivering. I lower the jug again and pour more water for them. And a third time.

Oh, to be a goat with nothing more to think about than eating and drinking and sleeping!

I scratch a head, and pat a couple of backs, feeling the tight, curly hair under my fingers. The afternoon sun warms their hair. The goats talk to me in their own way, bobbing and shaking their heads. And a couple watch me as I fill the jug one last time, and pour its contents into my own water jug, then head for my cottage. Carefully I close the gate to their field.

That's when I notice two young women, one with a babe on her hip. They walk toward me. The other woman, holding a boy toddler by the hand, walks with a limp.

The woman with the limp, face stark, asks, "Is it true? Did the Romans crucify him yesterday?"

I nod. I can't bring myself to say the words, but yes it is true.

"Everyone at temple is talking about it. About the priests sealing the tomb and placing guards at it," she says. Her cheeks are moistened by a sheen of tears. "We hoped it was not true."

I'm shocked at the news of guards. I could understand if the Romans had placed guards.

But the priests? Such dark mysteries make my head ache.

"You knew him?" I ask, having never seen either woman among Yeshua's followers.

"Oh, yes, we were baptized with him in the River Jordan," the woman with the infant says. "To us, he is our special treasure, although our father thinks he is a rabble rouser and warned us that he would come to no good end."

Then she pauses. Birds are singing with abandon and the pool of early spring sunlight that we stand in is unusually warm.

"Forgive our bad manners," she says. "I am Hannah and this is my sister Selah. We are of the house of Jeremiel. From Cana. Well, my sister is now of the house of Bariah, also in Cana." They look at me with soft eyes. "We're here for Passover. Staying with family."

She hands Selah the baby, who is beginning to squirm. She switches hands with the toddler, letting the little boy stand closer to the goat pasture fence.

"You were baptized with Yeshua?" I ask, surprised. I knew his cousin was the baptizer John, but I had not heard about Yeshua's baptism.

Hannah's face brightens. She and Selah nod.

"Our father had been very unhappy because he had no sons. Four daughters and no sons. And so, he made us all go hear John at the Jordan. He said that we must all be baptized for the remission of sins. He thought that someone in the household had sinned and grieved God. He said we must cleanse ourselves so that God would bless our house with a son."

I stare at the women. Clearly their family has status. Gold threads weave beautiful designs on their tunics. And gold bracelets fill their wrists. Their head scarves are of fine silk, billowing gently in the afternoon breeze.

"That was more than three years ago," Selah says softly. "And see," she motions to the toddler and the infant in her arms, who has settled down, "two sons since then. Two little brothers for us."

I never even wondered about Yeshua's baptism. Never thought about his life before he changed mine. Now I'm eager to hear.

"Were there many people at the Jordan?" I ask.

"Oh yes!" Selah says. "A multitude. It was like a festival, but a serious festival. People were there to confess their sins."

75

Hannah adds, "And John was preaching and everyone was jostling to get to the edge of the river. As soon as someone was baptized and walked out of the water, new people walked in. It was a clear day with lots of sun, the light sparkling off the river making us all squint."

Selah hands the infant back to Hannah, and helps the toddler reach through the fence, to coax the goats over for a pat.

"People would wade out into the water, and then sort of squat down until they were immersed," Hannah says. "That was baptism. You were supposed to repent, then wade out into the river and be washed free of sin."

Hanna places the baby back in Selah's arms. Selah's face crinkles with love as she smiles at the energetic infant. Then she grins, "This little fellow seems happiest if he's being passed around. So we keep him moving and then he doesn't cry."

She takes up the topic of baptism again. "Just as we reached the river's edge, so did Yeshua the Nazarene. He was right there, right beside me with the water splashing against his legs like it was splashing against mine." Selah turns to Hannah. "Remember that? How we all stepped into the water at the same time."

"Yes, and John looked so surprised when he saw Yeshua. They're cousins you know. And John was shocked; his eyes grew very large and he shook his head 'no.' And Yeshua held up his hand, as if to say, 'Just a minute, John.' Then he turned to us and told us to go first. Remember that?"

Selah almost laughs. "He was so gentle and yet so strong. It was as if he knew we needed to be baptized. We went as a complete family. All four of us girls and our father and mother and our servants. Everyone. Our whole household waded out together in one big company and then went under the river's flow.

"I remember how cold the water was and thinking that all my sins were being washed away, and that now perhaps father would have the son he longed for."

The toddler squeals in delight as a goat nuzzles his hand. Selah ruffles the hair on the child's head.

Hannah takes up the story. "We waded back to shore together, passing Yeshua as he moved deeper into the river. He smiled at us like we were old friends."

Selah adds, "John kept protesting, saying that Yeshua ought to baptise him not the other way around, but they talked together like cousins will, and when we reached the bank and looked back, Yeshua was going under the water."

The two women bow their heads as if in prayer, as if something special is about to be shared.

"And then the most amazing thing happened," Hannah says and she and Selah both grin and nod as if they still can't believe what they're about to tell me.

"Yeshua came straight up out of the water and it was as if everything – the wind and the flow of the river and all the people milling about and everything simply stopped. As if we were all frozen, just standing there staring at Yeshua. And the sky broke open like an egg. And through the open crack, a waterfall of light poured right down on him. A bright stream straight from heaven to him, light glinting off the water and shining off his shoulders and wet hair. He wiped the water out of his eyes and there was a radiance, a little glowing half circle like a rainbow around his head. And then, and then the whitest dove you've ever seen flew down and hovered above him."

Both women look at me, their eyes earnest. I try to picture what they're describing.

"And then the dove landed on his shoulder. Its wings fluttered a little, like they do when they land. And the dove and Yeshua stood there in the shimmering light."

Hannah continues, "That's when we heard God speak. Believe me, I'm telling you it was the voice of The Almighty. The words rang like music. They came down right out of the sky, like the light and the dove, and they filled the whole river valley: 'This is my beloved Son in whom I am well pleased.'"

Selah's dark eyes brim with joy at the memory. "Can you imagine being baptized and just moments later hearing the voice of God? Now our father insists it was lightning and thunder. An afternoon storm. But there were no clouds on that clear, sunny day. And thunder does not roar in words we can understand."

I'm astonished. I've never heard this story. And I'm with two women who were actually there, actually baptized with Yeshua and who heard the voice of God proclaim him Son.

"Oh!" I gasp, joy rushing through me. "Oh! I love your story. You've made me so happy in sharing it. This is the best thing I've heard all day."

My tears rise, but I catch myself before I sob. "It's been such a nightmare," I whisper. "I can hardly bear that he's gone. But you have given me something beautiful to hold in my heart."

Hannah says, "Yes. It was beautiful. A miracle. We must hold to that now."

I wipe my eyes. "Meeting you like this, hearing your story, this is a gift," I say as the sun slips behind some clouds and the resulting chill begins to reach through my tunic and shawl. I pull the shawl tighter.

"So you can see why he is special to us," Hannah says.

"And there is more," Selah adds.

I need to get back to the cottage, but I don't want to part with these women.

"A few of Yeshua's women followers are in my cottage," I nod in its direction. "We're honoring his memory and comforting one another. Would you join us? Could you? It would be a blessing if you would share the story."

The sisters consider my invitation and pass the infant again. "We will have to ask," Selah says. "And I have another story about our special Yeshua that you might love. It is joyous. But we have to have father's permission; we really shouldn't be out here this long."

I point again down the hill toward my cottage. "If you'd like, I'll wait for you." I say. They both nod assent and head back to the house where they're staying. Selah's limp is more noticeable now that I'm paying attention.

Soon they're back. "We may visit but only for a few minutes, " Selah says.

I can sense that she's heard about my reputation. It shows on her face. She looks both embarrassed and sympathetic at the same time.

All I know is that I'm grateful for the blessing of these sisters on the absolute worst day of my life.

Selah limps beside me. Hannah walks on her other side. I match my gait to Selah's. "God has blessed me," she says, holding what I now notice as her pregnant belly. "Perhaps my first-born will be a son. And if it is, I shall name him Yeshua, as a thank you."

We walk in silence. I think about Yeshua's baptism. If God loved him so, how could he allow what happened yesterday? But as quickly as the question fills my mind, I try and banish it.

At the cottage I introduce Selah and Hanna and explain that they were baptized with Yeshua in the River Jordan.

All eyes turn eagerly to the sisters and everyone insists on hearing the story, so the two repeat what they told me. And as their beautiful story unfolds, I watch the sad faces relax, open, smile. The story softens our grief.

When Hannah finishes the tale, Martha passes them both a basket of fruit and Joanna hands each a slice of honeycomb. The room quiets, as we wait for them to enjoy their repast, and continue their story.

"We are so sad that the Romans killed him," Hannah says.

Selah covers her face. "I can't believe it," her voice quavers.

My own heart joins her. How could The Almighty permit it? The question haunting me is wrapped in mystery. I feel as if we women have been together, mourning, forever. I feel exhausted. Old. Ready for the grave.

Selah regains her composure. "Please forgive me," she whispers. "I'm not allowed to show such feelings in front of my father. To him, we are here for Passover, our joyous Festival of Freedom, and nothing else must fill our heart."

She clears her throat and smiles shyly. "Thank you for understanding."

I remember she said she had another Yeshua story, and ask her to share it.

"Yes, I have another Yeshua story," she says, "A happy story, although it starts out sad."

Taking a deep breath, she leans back against the wall, and begins. "I was my father's first born child. And I was born with a short leg. He felt God had punished him by making his firstborn a crippled girl.

"Because of my leg, I could not do the normal chores. Could not draw and carry water. Could not harvest reeds for my mother's baskets. And my father was certain no one would want me for a wife.

"As you know, most of us are betrothed by the time of our menstrual periods. But no one approached my father for me." She pauses, and

I feel her disappointment. "However, shortly after our family baptism, that changed. Elhanan, the second son of Bariah, asked for me. Well, more accurately, Elhanan and his father asked for me. They had also been at the River Jordan and had seen us all baptized. Elhanan was also baptized that day. My father and Elhanan's father worked out the agreement. I believe it shocked my father that a family of such standing — their flocks and herds are known everywhere — would desire his crippled daughter. But I was pleased. Our betrothal was shorter than usual. Both families were eager for the union.

"Our wedding went well. The torch light procession led by Elhanan, the trip back to Bariah's home, being escorted to the bridal chamber. It was," her eyes sparkle at the memory and her face flushes. "Well, I'm sure you all know how wonderful that is. Such a perfect beginning…." she pauses as if deep in thought.

"The wedding feast was a big one. Almost the whole of Cana came to celebrate. And it turns out that Yeshua's mother is related to Bariah."

Several women ask, "Really?"

"Yes, she was helping with the feast. She was in charge of fruit and drinks. Oh, the food was so wonderful. Even though I was not supposed to be out of the chamber, I sneaked out with an attendant now and then. Of course, servants brought trays of delicious fare to my chamber. Baked sardines in Tahini sauce. Dolmas. Roast duck with mulberries. Sweet millet fruit balls. Cakes drenched in grape syrup."

My mouth waters as Selah recalls the many delicacies served at her marriage feast.

"On the third day of this perfect wedding feast, tragedy struck. Elhanan confided in me that his father had run out of wine."

We gasp and eyes meet all around. A feast of the size Selah is describing would be legendary. The family's reputation and the future of the young couple depend on a successful feast. To run out of wine is unheard of.

"How could it happen?" someone asks.

Selah shakes her head. "There were many complications according to Elhanan. His father had ordered what he estimated was more than enough. But there was a problem with transportation. Only part of the order was delivered. And then Yeshua arrived with several of his fisherman disciples and you know a fisherman's appetite for food and drink."

Spontaneous laughter fills room. Several women laugh so hard, they cover their faces.

Someone says, "Well, that certainly explains it."

Yes, we all know the bigger-than-life appetites of the disciples. No matter how much food and wine you set before them, they can devour it all quickly and still have room for more.

"Elhanan came to my chamber to tell me everything and to be sad with me. This tragedy would bring great shame both to his family and to our union. He and I would have to live with that shame.

"But, well," the color rises in her cheeks again. "Whenever he came to my chamber, we could not feel sad for long. And even though the wine was gone, there was beautiful music. We could hear the tambourines and the strings. We could hear the dancing. So, we were concerned, of course, but we could not be unhappy. "

I pass the food baskets around, feeling a little lighter as I listen to Selah describe such love.

"After Elhanan returned to the feast, my attendant and I went to the food preparation area, thinking we might be able to find wine that others had overlooked. You know how sometimes things get set aside and then seem lost, even though they're simply misplaced?

"I know I was not supposed to be seen, but I just had to help in any way I could, and I kept myself fully shrouded so that even if someone looked my way, they wouldn't recognize me."

She smiles and some of us actually laugh at her joke. Obviously, some in the room remember how curious they were during their wedding feasts, while they were supposed to be shut up in their chambers. They remember venturing out, too, and, evidently, the memories are pleasant.

"I was thrilled when I saw Yeshua and his mother over by the fruit peeling station. You know, she's a very tiny lady. But you can see that she is strong as an oak. Her arms and hands have power in them. I'd like to look like her when I'm her age. And she has an assurance about her. Well, just look at the son she raised! You can easily tell, when she takes charge, she takes charge.

"I'm sure she was explaining the wine problem to him. I couldn't hear them, but she pointed to the empty wine containers and it was clear that he was listening closely to her. He reached down and gently brushed some stray hairs off her forehead. It was such a loving gesture. Then he went back into the feast hall. She walked in my direction where the servants were artfully arranging dried apricots and raisins and dates on serving platters.

"I heard her say to them, 'Do whatever he tells you.' And I wondered what Yeshua would tell them to do. I stayed out of sight, of course. But I wanted to hear what Yeshua would say to them. However, let me assure you, my attendant and I also continued searching, looking under tables and behind curtains, seeing if we could find any hidden wine. No luck. But, oh, the fragrances that filled the air – the baking lamb and roasting duck. Mmmmm. I loved being surrounded with all that food, knowing that everyone was celebrating Elhanan and me and our marriage.

"The entire place was delicious … and I could hear the music, and the happy voices, the laughter and chatter from the feast hall. My heart felt like it would burst, but I knew catastrophe would soon overtake joy."

She pauses, pushes her head veil off and runs her hands through her hair. "And then,

Yeshua brushed past me. Like he was on a mission. He walked over to the servants standing near six stone water-jars, the kind used for rites of purification. He and the servants talked about the jars. I saw him look into each one as if he was looking down a deep well. Evidently, they were empty. He said to the servants, 'Fill the jars with water. Fill them up.'

"Obediently they went back and forth from the well to the jars, back and forth, back and forth, filling them with water. It took quite a while. The servants were dripping in sweat by the time all six jars were full. And all that time, I was watching Yeshua and remembering the water in the Jordan and sharing an afternoon in the river together having our sins washed away.

"As each jar filled, Yeshua looked at the water and nodded. 'Good, very good,' he would say. Then he would thank the servants and send them to fill the next jar. When the last jar was full to the brim, he said, 'Now draw some off and take it to the steward of the feast.' The servant whose silver dipper drew off the water looked like he'd seen a ghost.

"His eyes were wide and he stared at the full dipper and then at Yeshua. And Yeshua was all smiles. In fact, I think he was chuckling as he nodded, urging the servant to take the dipper of water to the steward.

"As the servant passed me, I glanced at the water in the dipper and it was no longer water. It was wine."

A gasp goes up from the entire room. Then the women start to laugh. "Wine?" several ask.

Selah nods, her own eyes dancing. "Yeshua changed six water-jars almost as tall as I am, six water-jars full of water into wine for my wedding feast.

"The man blessed by God at the River Jordan blessed my marriage. And saved my family's honor."

She's smiling. "It was the finest wedding gift imaginable. And he looked so happy to be giving it." Her hand covers her mouth as a giggle escapes. "And it was very good wine. Everyone commented on it. They were all saying how surprising it was that the family saved the best wine for last."

Selah's story elicits murmuring and laughter, a cottage full of pleasure.

"You see why Yeshua is so special to me," her red-rimmed eyes now sparkle. "Twice our paths have crossed and both times I feel as if YHWH Himself has touched my life with blessings."

I look at this young woman and am so grateful to have met her and to have heard her wonderful stories of my beloved teacher.

She gazes around the room, then says, "Thank you. For encouraging me to share. It has helped me feel a little better. I'm not allowed to speak of such things in the presence of my father. But today, knowing what was done to my precious Yeshua, I thank you for letting me share these memories. Now we must return to our family."

Before they leave, Mary and Martha, Joanna and Suzanna embrace the sisters. Words of "Thank you. Thank you." follow them out the door.

I marvel at the fresh air feeling they brought to our gathering.

Late afternoon shadows climb the walls of nearby houses as I shut the window-covering lattice and light an oil lamp. Several of the women have left. Those who remain don't seem inclined to go. Their soft voices fill my cottage.

In the gentle lull, a woman quite a bit younger than I am, stout and with straight brown hair gathered at the nape of her neck, begins to speak. Her soft voice reveals her shyness. When I ask her to speak a little louder so we can all hear what she has to say, she blushes.

"I am so grateful for this gathering, for being here today," she says, brushing back a few stray strands of hair. "I also have a story, a very plain story, but I need to share it because I think it says so much about him."

Everyone says, "Yes. Yes. We want to hear."

"It is a simple story," she says almost apologetically. "You may recognize yourself in it because it is a story of women's work. Our never-ending work." She hesitates as if organizing her thoughts.

I wonder what her story is.

"I was making bread. Such a common task. I get so tired of doing it. Grinding the barley into flour. Grinding and grinding. Then adding a little water until it becomes dough. And then kneading and kneading. It's all so . . . tedious. But it must be done. We must have bread to live. Almost every day I make my barley loaves. Small, brown, boring."

A group chuckle rises at her description. We know well what she means.

"In our neighborhood we share the ovens. And on this particular day, I was the first to use one. I had gathered the necessary dung to fire up the oven and keep the fire constant. I was so tired of the never ending task of it all that my heart just wasn't in it.

"But, my husband and I have one son. Benjamin is the light of our life. He is such a good boy with the sweetest spirit. Soon he will turn nine.

"So, to keep from getting too bored, I focused on him, thinking, I'm making this bread for our Ben. As I ground the barley and worked it into dough, I added a little olive oil. Just for a slightly different flavor. Something special for my special boy.

"And as I shaped the dough and placed it along the walls of the hot oven, I kept thinking how my son would enjoy it. You know how you must keep turning the bread, and keep tending the fire so that everything comes out right.

"By thinking about Ben I was able to work in the morning's growing heat without becoming, how can I say it, irritated with the monotony of it all. Little did I know that the bread I made with love would find its way into the blessed hands of Yeshua."

She pauses, and I'm eager to hear more. "Go on," several women say.

"The very next day, my boy came running into the house shouting, 'Yeshua is here! Yeshua is here!' My husband, who had just milked the goats and was getting ready to take them out to pasture, grabbed him up in his arms and said, 'What's this about the great Yeshua?'

"You see, we'd heard of his teachings and talked at length together about him. A cousin living closer to Galilee told us about Yeshua's wonderful works, how he heals the sick and says that the Kingdom of God is at hand. Benjamin and some of his friends have imagined what they would do if they had a chance to meet Yeshua.

"'I would ask him to bless me,' our son had said, 'and bless our family.' My husband and I had laughed, delighted at his good heart.

"Actually, my husband often says that our son has the generous heart and sweet disposition of his mother." She blushes again. I can tell she appreciates such loving words from her man.

"So our boy was all excited about Yeshua being on the outskirts of our village. 'He's going to teach us,' Ben said. 'I want to hear his teaching.'

"My husband lifted our son up to his shoulders and headed out to see for himself. In a few minutes he was back. 'There's quite a crowd,' he said. 'Yeshua is not with them, but they know where he is going to be this afternoon and they're all heading out to meet him there. My brother is among them. If you want to take the boy and go hear what Yeshua has to say, my brother will let you walk with him.'

"'Please, Mama, please!' Ben was jumping up and down.

"I quickly gathered several of the barley loaves I'd made the day before, and a couple of dried fish so that we'd have something to eat if the gathering lasted too long. You know how hungry little boys can get." she says.

"And big boys too," one of the women says. Everyone chuckles.

"So, we hurried out to join the crowd. Holding Ben's hand and carrying the basket of bread, I felt suddenly grateful that I'd baked the loaves.

"We walked a long way, past farms and a small village, around Lake Galilee, and ended up in a lovely, wide meadow not far from the lake. Long grass and lots of pretty wildflowers surrounded us. A fragrant breeze kept the temperature bearable. Thank goodness I had my brother-in-law to help with our boy."

Someone asks, "Did Yeshua see you? Did he notice you?"

"I don't think so," she says. "He and his disciples were teaching those who had arrived earlier. Because I'm short and my boy is not yet tall, I urged my brother-in-law to lead us to the front of the crowd, and he did. From there, we could easily see and hear Yeshaua."

She pauses. "He spoke of love and his voice was beautiful. I could have listened to it for weeks. He spoke of God's kingdom of peace and goodness. The hours passed quickly. I tried to hold on to his words so that I could take them home to my husband.

"And then, he stopped teaching and turned to his disciples. He said, 'We must feed these people. It's supper time. They're hungry.' I'll always remember the look on his face and the sound of his voice.

"He cared that people were growing hungry. Of course, we were all hungry for his words, for his truth, for his teaching. But he cared about our growling stomachs. It seemed so, so unusually kind of him.

"And his disciples were all in a dither about feeding the crowd, protesting they didn't have enough money to buy food. And we were way out in the middle of nowhere. They said that Yeshua should pray a blessing and send us all back to our homes.

"But Yeshua would not hear of it. He acted like a caring host. As if he had invited us to his home and was now going to serve us a meal. He said, 'Have the people sit down.' So the disciples began organizing us all. They had us sit in rows of about, I don't know, maybe 50 or 100. As we sat down, they were asking if anyone had food they could share.

"Pointing at our little basket, Ben said, 'We have food.'

"My brother-in-law hushed him, saying 'If you give them our food, we'll have nothing. There's barely enough for us.' My son looked at me with pleading eyes. 'Please!'

"I could see that it meant the world to him to give Yeshua what he'd asked for. I handed him the basket. As he ran up to the disciples,

I turned to my brother-in-law. 'It's the chance of his young lifetime to actually give something to Yeshua. If they can use our little offering, I think we can skip supper without suffering too much.' He just rolled his eyes.

"Soon Ben was back. 'They took it!' he said, grinning. 'They took our supper to Yeshua. They said something like, 'The boy only has five small barley loaves and two fish. But what is that with so many here?' Yeshua looked inside the basket and then he looked at me, right at me, Mama, and he smiled and nodded.' Benjamin's mouth was wide open in delight. 'He smiled and nodded to me. Like he said thank you to me!'

"I hugged him tight. He had actually given Yeshua a gift. Then I realized that so had I, for I had made the bread."

She wipes her eyes before continuing. "We're just common people, my husband and I. And my bread was just common barley. But Yeshua took it and thanked my son for it.

"When the disciples were getting everyone seated, some of them went down to a boat at the edge of the sea. They came back with their arms full of large baskets.

"With everyone seated, and the disciples back from the boat, Yeshua stared for a long moment into our little basket, then raised his face toward heaven and gave thanks for the food my dear son had brought to him. After his prayer, he began to break the bread and the fish into bite-sized pieces. And as he broke the food, he filled the disciples' baskets and the disciples passed the baskets along the rows of people. Basket after basket of bread and fish, and Yeshua kept breaking our little offering."

Her eyes beam despite their tears. "Can you believe it?" she shakes her head in wonderment. "My humble barley loaves in his hands became a summer evening feast, with the birds singing nearby and the breeze mussing our hair."

"We heard about that wondrous act," several women say. "We heard there were 5,000 people fed that day, but we didn't know if it was true."

"Oh, it was true," the woman says. "But the 5,000 were just the men. They only counted the men. There were hundreds, maybe thousands of children, and women. The crowd filled the whole wide meadow almost all the way to the lake.

"As I watched Yeshua break my barley loaves into enough food for everyone, I thought of God providing manna in the desert for our ancestors. I realized I was seeing God's kingdom come, just as Yeshua has said. It took hours for him to fill those baskets with bread and fish. The sun was setting by the time he finished and the disciples wandered among us, gathering the leftovers.

"My sweet boy had dreamed of asking Yeshua to bless our family, and instead Yeshua had used him and my loaves to bless the people there." Tears continue to flow down her cheeks. "I can't tell you all the feelings I had witnessing Yeshua's loving act and realizing the part we had in it."

She shakes her head.

Her story has lifted my spirits. Her words transported me, and I'm sure all the others, to another time and place filled with grace.

"Just one more thing," she says. "Watching Yeshua fill the baskets with my humble barley loaves, I realized that he can do amazing things with just ordinary stuff. His love, his caring action that afternoon changed my outlook on life. I doubt I'll ever again feel that making bread is tedious work."

CHAPTER 6

DINNER PARTY AT BETHANY

Martha and I pass the food baskets again. The cottage is quiet as we eat, each considering her own thoughts and memories.

In the gentle silence, my heart begins to relax. For a few minutes I feel almost normal. Thoughts of my family back in Magdala tiptoe in. I wonder if they have heard about yesterday. Word is not likely to have reached my father or the many workers in his fish salting business. Most of his workers are Gentiles, so he has no need to shut the business down for Passover.

Even as a child, I understood that he was not interested in temple or Torah. The only thing that has ever been important to him is making money, and he couldn't make money if he closed down the operation for several days. I'm sure he and my brothers (who have adopted his view of what counts in life) are running the business as usual and know nothing of the brutal loss we've suffered here.

But my mother and her sisters, who weave and dye fine fabric for Uncle Yakov's shops, are likely to hear about the execution through their many connections, or from their friends who have journeyed to Jerusalem for Passover. They will know soon enough.

I can see my mother's sad face, as she accepts the fact that for yet another year she will remain at home in Magdala instead of celebrating Passover at Jerusalem's stunning temple. However, I'm glad she has been spared what the rest of us are going through. Her heart is not yet bleeding.

I realize how much I miss my kind and patient mother. I wish she were with me now. But it's a blessing she isn't. A temporary blessing of ignorance.

Running my hand over the rug beneath me, I think of Magdala and long for the soft, swishy, intoxicating sound of waves lapping the sea shore, the shore where I splashed and played as a child. There is much I miss today about my childhood home, but I don't miss the smell of fish drying in the sun. And I don't miss the sadness that so often filled our home. A feeling like rain clouds that never drop their burden.

The last time I saw my parents was on a mountainside, not far from town. Yeshua had been teaching in the nearby synagogues, healing the sick, and enjoying the fellowship of fishermen and others beside the Sea of Galilee. Crowds were following him, eager to hear his words and hoping to see a miracle.

On this particular day, he left town, hiking through the Valley of Doves and then up the mountain. It was a breezy day filled with sunshine and white round clouds. When he reached the top, he sat down, and all the people gathered near. My father and mother were there. I had begged them more than once to attend his gatherings. Seeing them there was a great boon to me. I sat with them on the thick, sweet smelling grass. From our vantage point, we could see the sea and its lively waves. An invigorating view. My father seemed to approve of Yeshua's words when he said, "Repent for the Kingdom of Heaven is upon you."

But when Yeshua began pronouncing his blessings with, "Blessed are the poor for theirs is the kingdom of heaven," my father grew agitated, even angry.

"He's contradicting King Solomon's Proverbs," he said to my mother. And then he quoted: "The blessing of the Lord makes a person rich. Wealth is a crown for the wise."

I was surprised that father knew any scripture passages. But I could see his disapproval of Yeshua's words as he fidgeted and whispered angrily to my mother. I so wanted for them to hear and see in Yeshua, the Promised One that I had come to know. When Yeshua pronounced, "Blessed are the meek for they shall inherit the earth," father stood up, cursing under his breath. Pulling my mother up beside him, he stomped away shaking his head in disgust. Poor mother having to tag along with an angry husband.

My heart ached as I watched them heading back toward town. If only they could have heard Yeshua's message of compassion and reassurance like I heard it, a love-filled, hope-filled message. The memory of my father stamping down the mountain that afternoon, pulling my mother with him, is like a boulder in my stomach. Its heaviness brings me back to my present pain

— to the realization that I will never again hear Yeshua's voice.

Two women thank me for the day and depart. Imma makes her way to my side. "Do not hate me for what I said," she whispers as she embraces me, then kisses both my cheeks.

"We are all mixed up today," I whisper back. "Filled with confusion and…"

"Fear," she finishes my sentence.

I realize that these dear sisters need to feel they are not totally lost in this evil world. "Listen," I say to those still in the room, "until we can figure out what to do, let's meet together here once a week. How does that sound?" Heads bob assent. "We can strengthen one another with our company."

My idea seems to strike a chord. There's quite a discussion about what day to meet and, eventually, we all settle on Sabbath. Following services.

I say, "Those of us not normally in Jerusalem on Sabbath can come by any time. I would love your company."

Even though women have come and gone all day, and more have trickled out as the afternoon has lengthened, my cottage still seems full to bursting.

My thoughts turn to last week's dinner party in Bethany. Only a week ago! Seems like a lifetime. Who could have imagined then what we are going through now?

When I'd heard that Mary and Martha were planning a gratitude party for our beloved teacher, I wanted more than anything to be part of it, to add my own "thank you" to the event.

I asked to serve at the dinner. But Martha and three others were serving. Lazarus and Mary would host. So I went home to ponder what I could do that others were not doing. How could I express my gratitude for all he had given me: new life, new purpose, and the blessed certainty that he was the Promised One. I recalled his praise for the elderly widow who dropped two mites — all she had — into the Temple offering box. Clearly he treasures a generous heart.

How could I be generous? What could I give? I poured the contents of my savings pouch onto my table and was surprised at how much I had. As I considered my pile of shiny coins, the thought of anointing arose within me. It appeared that I had enough for a flask of pure ointment of Spikenard. What better gift than something symbolizing the royal and the sacred?

I spent two entire mornings at market searching for just the right flask. I enjoy the market, its noise and clutter, the vegetable booths and the fabric booths, the tables of bread, the booths of slippers and scarves. I stopped often, savoring the sights and smells and sounds, examining every flask in every booth until I finally found the perfect one — alabaster, with a long, graceful neck and a softly rounded base. Its creamy-ivory color held streaks of gold so that when the light struck it just right it sparkled.

It took all my coins to buy it and fill it with the thick, amber colored ointment. All the way home, I sneaked sniffs, happy that I could actually give him something so deliciously beautiful. Its fragrance filled me with a sense of deep satisfaction.

Spikenard is more than just a perfume. Some use it as a medicine. It is also recognized as a sedative, able to bring the body to a state of peacefulness. It is one of the eleven herbs used for incense in the Holy Temple. It is legendary, the perfect gift.

How would he react when I'd start to anoint his feet? Would he jerk away and say, "Stop, it tickles!" I smiled at the thought. I would use firm, long strokes so that the soothing balm would easily absorb and relax him.

By the time I arrived at the party, the house was full, with everyone eating and laughing. The clink of glasses and dishes. The room full of stories as the men tried to outdo each other with their tales. Although I'd been eager to get there, I suddenly felt shy. Martha immediately came to me. She must have seen me, standing just inside the door searching the room for him.

"Follow me," she said. "He's on the other side."

Then I saw him, reclining on one of the dinner couches, talking enthusiastically with those near him. His strong square hands were weaving designs in the air as he spoke. I followed Martha, trying to be invisible, until I was standing right behind him, my back against the wall; my flask nestled tightly to my chest.

The bowls and platters, heaped with food, came in an unending parade, as the empty plates were carried away. Lazarus and other servers kept the wine flowing.

When I was as close to invisible as I could get, I knelt at the foot of his couch. He glanced over his shoulder at me. His dark, cheerful eyes under their bushy brows held me for just a second and in that second the word "Shalom" filled me and I felt so totally accepted that tears rose.

Carefully rolling back his gown so that his ankles and feet were fully revealed, I could not stop my tears. All this man had given me — a sense of forgiveness, a sense of acceptance, a sense of belonging, a sense of purpose — rushed to the surface and my tears became a warm stream, washing the dust from his feet. It was natural to bend close and kiss those precious feet. I pressed my lips against the base of his heal. First his left foot, then his right. It may sound strange, but when I kissed his feet, I felt as if he were my child, an innocent one whom I wished to love and care for. He wiggled his toes ever so slightly. I thought that simple movement was a "thank you" message sent from his good heart. Then, using my hair as a towel, I dried his feet with as much care as I could.

While I worked, I prayed for God's blessing on him. Then, I removed the stopper from my flask and poured out the thick, silky contents, carefully massaging the fragrant ointment into his skin.

I could tell his feet appreciated what I was doing by the way they soaked up the ointment. As if they were sun-parched, dust-drenched and thirsty beyond measure. The Nard smoothed his travel-weary skin, transforming the rough spots to a buttery leather feel.

I was lost in the action as my fingers slipped over his ankles and feet, massaging the muscles and tendons, pressing and kneading. The hair on his legs surprised me. It was dark and thick as a blanket. I hoped my touch and the lotion were relaxing and refreshing him. I thought at one point I heard a contented sigh escape his lips.

I had not counted on how fully the fragrance would permeate the room. Soon I felt other eyes glancing my way, some curious, some disapproving. I focused on smoothing and massaging the cream into his strong, sturdy feet.

Perhaps it was my imagination, but it seemed that the entire room quieted a little as if a sort of fresh yet earthy-smelling shalom was settling on everyone, as if my gift to him was giving all the dinner guests a moment of repose.

Then I heard the reed-thin voice of Judas rise in complaint. "Do you realize how many poor people she could have fed with the money spent on that Nard?" Glancing up, I saw him looking for agreement from the others. "What's the cost now? A hundred denari for enough Nard to fill the palm of my hand? Talk about extravagance. Surely she could have saved three-hundred pieces of silver for the ointment she's used so far. "

The calm brought on by the rich fragrance disappeared as the men began calculating the cost of what I was doing. And how much good my money could have done for the poor. And how much I was wasting while the poor suffered. I poured the last few fat drops into my hand, set the flask down on the floor next to his sandals, and carefully massaged his soles. Then I stood up and backed away.

"Stop complaining," Yeshua said to the others around the table. "She's done a beautiful thing for me. She has anointed my body for burial."

Now, in my cottage full of sisters, I suddenly hear his words distinctly, much more distinctly than I'd heard them that night. "She's done a beautiful thing for me. She has anointed my body for burial."

He knew what lay ahead!

I had imagined anointing him as my king . . . I'd imagined rubbing all the ache and tiredness out of his feet . . . I'd imagined telling him through my touch and the ointment's rich balm that I love his teachings and would always follow them. Yet he knew what he was facing and he saw my act as preparation for the tomb.

Now I sob openly. He knew what was coming, and still he could enjoy a dinner with friends and look at me with happiness and acceptance.

Joanna sees my tears, brushes back my hair, and runs her cool hand across my forehead. I am grateful for her presence. Grateful that I'm not alone today. Looking at the others, I see in them the grief coursing through me. And yet, here we are, together, trying our best to make some sense of it all, and failing.

By sunset we are totally talked out. Cried out.

Together, we perform the end-of-Sabbath rituals. Together recite the Havdalah prayer. But there is no leave-taking. It's as if no one wishes to venture out into reality. I turn up the light in my oil lamp. The soft flicker of its flame adds a warm glow to the faces gathered here.

He has been gone an entire Sabbath.

Then a thought settles among us. Joanna and Leah mention it simultaneously. Even though we can change nothing about yesterday's atrocity at Golgotha, we can do something for Yeshua. We can give our Teacher, our Promised One, a proper burial. Joseph and Nicodemus wrapped him in linen, but they didn't have time to properly prepare his precious body for burial. In the rush to place him safely in the tomb before the sacred Sabbath hours arrived, several important touches were ignored. Serving Yeshua in this way is the least we can do. And, obviously, it's the only thing we can do.

Taking the packet Uncle Yakov gave me, I divide its coins among four of the sisters. They leave immediately to buy the necessary spices and containers to hold the mixtures.

While we wait, it's agreed that Mary, the mother of James, and I will be the ones to go and anoint his body. The two of us had followed and provided for him since his very first days in Galilee. We heard all his teachings. And we know exactly where his tomb is.

The sisters who remain in my cottage promise to pray for us tomorrow as we perform the proper burial rites.

Since none of us can think of anything else we can do, we'll give this one, final gift to the man who brought us life abundant.

By the time the moon has risen, the women are back. Everyone has a hand in mixing the spices — myrrh, aloes, cassia, lavender and others. With loving fingers we crush and grind and blend in cold stone bowls. And from those bowls, sweet, spicy, calming aromas rise, filling the room. A soft, still sadness accompanies our work. We finish our task quietly and pour the bowls into proper pouches. Two very large and heavy pouches. Then we wait.

Joanna assures us that Chuza and his friends will come to walk everyone safely home. Eventually the men appear and after many tearful embraces, the remaining sisters leave.

Silence. My cottage is filled with desolate silence.

Despite the flickering lamplight and the spicy fragrance from the pouches on my table, I am gripped by the fist of loss.

Yeshua announced the arrival of God's kingdom. And then he showed us that kingdom through his words and deeds. Love. Peace.

Compassion. Forgiveness. And now he lies in that cold stone tomb.

I tidy the room, gather the left-overs and bread baskets, put away my Sabbath rugs.

Eventually I extinguish the lamp and sit in darkness trying to imagine life without him. Outside, rain drops tap mournfully on the roof. The wind sighs as it swirls leaves and dust along the street.

Today, with all the sisters, all the heartwarming stories, I felt almost reassured. Now, only despair.

Unrolling my sleeping mat and cover, I crawl inside.

CHAPTER 7

THE TOMB

Sleep comes, but it is intermittent. Every sound, no matter how slight — footsteps on the street, the wind rattling bushes — snaps my eyes open and sets my heart racing. I cower under my blanket, holding my breath, expecting a soldier to burst in at any moment.

And when I finally drift off, bloody scenes fill my head. Angry faces, angry voices, hammers pounding, blood spraying.

Eventually I give up, get up and prepare for the day. I step outside for a moment. Mist floats down like wistful tears. Turning my face to the sky, I welcome the night-cool moisture. In the darkness, the wet black street disappears between dark houses. I breathe deeply, letting the rain-washed air fill my lungs. How I wish the world was different than it is.

By the time Mary, James' mother, appears at my door, I'm dressed, with my hair braided and wound wreath-like about my head. I pour us a cup of water, which we drink in silence.

As we fasten our shawls and mantels and lift the heavy packets of burial spices to our shoulders, I ask, "Did you sleep well?"

She shakes her head. "It was impossible."

"Same for me."

"I'm thankful we're doing this together," she says. "I doubt I'd have the strength to do it by myself." Exactly how I feel.

The remains of last night's rain and this morning's mist drip from tree branches and roof edges. The dreary drizzle matches my mood. Yet I'm glad to be out with Mary, walking, moving, doing something besides weeping.

Somewhere in this soaking city, dogs bark.

Fear and sorrow weave an inner fabric that clenches my heart until it can barely beat. Still, we make our way through the damp streets. Soldiers stand at many corners. They look bored, or perhaps tired, but they represent the danger we all face. The disciples fled Friday. Will Rome find and crucify them next? Will Golgotha become a forest of crosses filled with

Yeshua's followers? If they believed Yeshua was a threat, how will the Gentile-Romans view us? I pull my shawl close with one arm, as I balance the pouch of spice with my other. Its sweet fragrance envelopes me, yet holds no comfort.

The sun, barely glimmering over the hills, sends ribbons of light through the trees and turns the damp, sandy earth into a glistening carpet.

I know the temple's gold walls are gleaming in these early morning rays, glowing like the throne of YHWH. Mary and I should be in the courtyard, listening to Yeshua's life-filled words instead of trudging toward his grave.

"I keep thinking about our last supper together," her words break into my dark thoughts and I am grateful. "The way he washed everyone's feet. Just like a wife or a slave. I mean, who else do you know, what man would humble himself like that and do women's work as if it was the most natural thing in the world?"

Her words remind me of how often Yeshua prepared meals and served them, or worked alongside the rest of us as we prepared and served the meals. With him there were no "more important" or "less important" people or

119

tasks. We all did everything together and it was wonderful. We sang together as we baked bread or chopped vegetables. And we all ate together too, men and women, unlike the usual men eat first tradition most of us grew up with.

"He lived his teachings. They weren't just words with him," Mary continues. "He taught that the first would be last and the last first, and then he, the teacher, the Promised One, knelt and did the work of a slave or a wife, washing the feet of every person there."

I remember the lively conversation just three nights ago between Yeshua and Peter. "And Peter got nowhere with his loud objections to the foot washing," I say.

"Oh, yes. You know Peter. Dramatics all the time. He should have gone into the theater instead of being a fisherman."

"But he wouldn't have eaten so well," I say and we chuckle. It feels good to have something to chuckle about.

"Peter must be suffering greatly," I add.

"As we all are," she replies.

This early in the morning, the street out of the city is nearly deserted. A few farmers and their heavily-loaded burros plod in the opposite direction. The burros' feet clip clop as they pass. A turtle dove's soft song tumbles down from the roof of a nearby building.

At the city gate, we stop to catch our breath and reposition our spice packet burden. I can tell that Mary is as fearful as I am.

"This is an honor," I say, trying to encourage us both. And yet, all our hopes and dreams are in that tomb. Dead. Just like our precious master.

She glances sideways at me, her tear-swollen eyes unconvinced.

"Our last chance to do anything for him," I continue, unable to bear the thought of his poor, abused body lying there neglected.

She whispers, "It's too sad to think about."

The sun's growing rays begin to dry yesterday's dusty coating on the city's sandstone walls. The powdery smell makes us both sneeze.

We start walking again. Golgotha, the barren skull-like hill of public execution, rises ahead to our right. As we turn toward the orchard graveyard at Golgotha's base where the new tomb holds our beloved Yeshua, she asks the question I've been pondering, "Who will move the stone for us?"

I've been dreading seeing his poor body, his bloodied and bruised head, wrapped in funeral linens. I, too, wonder about the boulder sealing the tomb.

"The guards. We'll ask the guards." I sound more confident than I feel. "We'll explain that we must properly care for his body, and surely they'll push the stone out of the way for us."

"What if they won't?" She fears, of course, that instead of helping us, they'll haul us off to the authorities.

"Well," I clear my throat, "then, we'll simply set our spices down and …" I see the tomb now, up ahead, and can't make sense of what I see. There are no guards. The entire area is empty. And silent. The huge boulder used as a seal has rolled or slid off to the side and the tomb's black doorway gapes like an open mouth. "Look!" I stop and stare. The doorway beckons, black and mysterious.

We quicken our pace. Has someone harmed Yeshua's precious body? We rush forward. Dropping our spices at the door, we stoop to enter. Our mantels fall. The tomb is still, dark, and cold. We catch our breath and let our eyes adjust. The place is empty. The stone body shelf, rising about three feet from the floor, holds nothing but neatly folded death linens. Confusion floods me. Where is his body? Where is he? As one, we step forward and touch the empty burial shelf. Its stony chill sends a shiver through me. Who took his body? Where could it be?

Before I can give voice to my questions, the chamber blazes with light so bright it hurts. Squinting between my fingers I see two men in dazzling apparel. They're standing right in front of us radiant as the sun. Our knees give out and we both sit with a thump onto the burial shelf. Terror rattles our teeth. We bend forward, pulling our shawls up over our heads and hiding our faces in our skirts. Are these the guards with some kind of miraculous torch? Even with my face buried, their light stabs my eyes.

"Why seek the living among the dead?" one says. His voice is rich and musical. I've never heard such a voice. It is definitely *not* human. My heart freezes in fear. I hold my breath. What have we stumbled into? The voice asks, "Did not he say that the Son of Man must be delivered into the hands of sinful men and be crucified and on the third day rise?"

The words weave through me like silken threads, creating a new pattern in my pain and grief. Yes, I remember those strange words from Yeshua. They made no sense at the time, and I simply forgot them. But now I remember.

"You seek Yeshua of Nazareth who was crucified," the two continue, their voices blending. Speaking in perfect unison they sound like an entire choir, or a musically flowing river. "But he has been raised. He is not here. Go tell his disciples and Peter that he is going to Galilee; there you will see him as he told you."

The blazing, blinding light is gone as suddenly as it appeared, leaving us shaken and alone in the blackness. Still perched on the shelf, we slowly straighten and lean against one another, trembling, not daring to stand just yet. Our eyes struggle to adjust. My mouth is dry as sand from my fearful gasping.

What just happened?

After a long time, we try to stand. Clinging to one another and leaning against the stone body shelf, we regain our feet. Reaching out to the wall to steady ourselves, we just stand there, shaking but upright.

Unsteady, we stagger outside. Her eyes are large as platters. I'm sure mine are too. We maneuver our spice-filled packages into the empty tomb. The effort strengthens us a little.

We walk like cripples, our arms around one another, as we turn and head out of the graveyard. Who were those beings? Were they angels? "Did we see two men in there?" I ask. Mary nods. "Do you think they were angels? Did they say Yeshua is risen?" She nods again, but her stunned face looks more like she's seen a ghost than an angel.

I had seen his broken body and bleeding wounds. I had seen him hanging limp on the cross, his chest neither rising nor falling. Could he be dead on Friday and alive today? Sunday? Is it possible?

Dazed and dazzled, we leave the cemetery behind and make our way through the city gate back the way we came. If those were angels, surely their words are true. Although confused, I feel a flicker of hope.

Could our beloved Promised One be alive? Oh, what a blessed thought!

We go directly to John's house and tell him and Yeshua's mother what happened at the tomb. Mother Mary listens, her eyes red-rimmed and brimming with tears, but she says nothing. When we repeat the words we heard in the tomb, that he is risen and is living and has gone ahead to Galilee, she closes her eyes and turns her face heavenward, her lips moving silently.

John gets us both a glass of water. We need it after the shock of the tomb. "The disciples and other followers are hiding in a house across town," John says. "I'll take you there."

We avoid main streets, staying as unobtrusive as possible. And as we walk, we try to figure out what the messengers in the tomb could have meant. Could Yeshua really be alive? It is impossible to believe. Yet, the speakers' musical voices and brilliant light seem impossible, too. And they were real. Hope glows within me like a tiny flame. Surely the disciples will be thrilled. I can't wait to tell them what we witnessed at the tomb — the empty tomb.

At the house, the owner quickly ushers us in, immediately shutting and bolting the door behind us. He leads us to a crowded inner room. The men hiding there all look like they've slept in their clothes. Hopelessness and fear cling to them like spider webs.

I recognize Peter at once and Philip and Matthew. We know these men and they know us. How many meals have we shared together? How many days have we spent listening to the wisdom and stories of our beloved Yeshua?

"Our sisters were at the tomb this morning," John says. "They witnessed something beyond comprehension and have come to share what they saw and heard."

James' mother stands beside me as I tell the rumpled, sad-eyed group about the two beings in the tomb, their brilliant light, their musical voices and their amazing words. My heart beats with hope as I describe the scene. Everyone leans forward to catch my words. But when I say, "They told us that Yeshua has risen and gone to Galilee," Peter and the others roll their eyes and throw their hands up.

They groan and wave their hands as if throwing my words back at me. It's as if they are saying, "Leave it to the women to concoct such an outrageous tale!"

"It's true," I insist. "They said we must tell you to meet Yeshua in Galilee." Before I can finish my sentence, they turn their backs to us.

127

"Listen," I plead. "This is what we saw. This is what we heard. You must meet him in Galilee." But they stare at the ceiling, shaking their heads in disgust and disbelief. I look at Mary standing beside me. She knows the truth I'm telling. She was there. But she's staring at the floor, totally mute. I look at John. He will not meet my eyes.

I cannot stand this room or the strangers in it any longer. Turning, I rush to the door, unbolt it and stumble out. My stomach is so knotted that I walk bent-over like an old woman. I pull my shawl tightly around me as if I'm in a windstorm.

I'm wretched, caught in an endless torment. Violence, hatred, blood, death and then an empty tomb ablaze with light and the words that our precious, beloved teacher is risen. What does it all mean? Nothing makes sense. I'm living in a nonstop nightmare. My head pounds. My chest aches. I am raw with loss and confusion.

Despite the soldiers patrolling the city, all I can think of is getting back to the tomb, back to the last place where Yeshua's precious body had been. I want to be where he had been laid. To simply be there, let my tears water the earth and my prayers fill the air.

When I arrive, out of breath, everything is exactly as we left it. Not a person in sight. Silent, empty tomb. Linens neatly folded. But no dazzling men with musical voices. Were they real? Did I really see and hear them? Or am I so broken by Yeshua's crucifixion that I have actually gone mad? If I could see those blazing beings again, I'd pepper them with questions.

I touch the cool linens, run my fingers along the cold limestone shelf, trying to feel where his body had lain. Opening the spice pouches we left in our rush to town, I sprinkle the spices all around the chamber and along the body shelf. Gathering up the neatly folded head linens, I bury my face in them. I inhale deeply, doing my best to breathe in his presence. Where is his body? Wrenching sobs rise from the depths of my heart. Where is he? What has happened here?

As the spices' fragrance fills the tomb, I drop the cloths and whisper prayers on his and our behalf. Memories of Yeshua flood me — his delight when mothers brought their babies and toddlers to him for blessing, his fiercely flashing eyes and powerful words when he threw over the money-changers' tables in the temple. And the gentleness in his voice after witnessing an elderly widow drop two mites into a temple collection box.

Memories of his lavish grace flood me and my heart aches at the loss of him. How can I, how can we go on without him?

Back outside, I wander among the older tombs and gnarled trees in blind confusion. He is gone and the disciples don't believe what I saw and heard. Not a word of it. And I can't make sense out of anything that's taken place since Friday. But the emptiness filling me is more than I can bear.

In the still morning air it feels like the world is holding its breath. I am lost. Shivering, I lean against an old, black oak and let the tears fall. My shaking sobs fill the air. I understand nothing that has happened in the last three days. Nothing.

"Oh, YHWH, God of my fathers, where are you now?"

A man's voice asks, "Why are you crying?"

Through my tears, I see who think is the gardener. Struggling to compose myself, I say, "Sir, they have taken away my lord and I don't know where they've laid him." Trying to steady my voice, I continue. "Please, if you have taken him, tell me where he is so I may minister to him."

He steps toward me and says one small word, "Mary."

A jolt of recognition shoots through me like a bolt of lightning. I recognize that voice. Shaking my head, rubbing my eyes, brushing away my tears, I stare intently at him. He is smiling. I know that smile. Those bushy eyebrows!

I can't believe my eyes. This isn't the gardener. It is Yeshua! How can that be? Standing before me in full health, no bruises, no bleeding. Looking like he's just arisen from a restful nap. How can it be? He is alive! And he is whole and well!

Wonder-struck, I face an unimaginable truth: The Almighty, the God of Heaven and Earth, has come to this place of death. And brought life.

Yeshua, my beloved teacher, is alive! Just like the dazzling beings with their musical voices said. It's too good to be true. But it is true. He is alive! His deep eyes glow. His face radiates love. I feel its warmth. He *is* alive!

"Rabboni!" I cry, falling at his feet, those feet I know so well. My arms encircle them in an eager, worshipful embrace. I feel like I'm in heaven. Our beloved Promised One is healthy and alive!

My hands grasp his ankles. I never want to let go. The bridges of his feet hold healed scars where just two days ago were vicious spikes. I kiss those scars with gratitude and my lips recognize the truth. Yeshua in flesh and blood is actually alive!

"Don't hold me, for I've not yet ascended to the Father," he says. "Go tell my brothers. Say that I'm ascending to my Father and your Father, to my God and your God."

I look up at that familiar face and think, *Another speaking assignment. The first time didn't go so well.*

His eyes twinkle as he nods ever so slightly. I suddenly want more than anything to tell the disciples that I have seen him, have heard his voice, have touched his lovely feet, and he is indeed alive. I want to tell all Jerusalem, all the world, that Yeshua is no longer dead. He has risen from the grave healthy and whole.

I hold his feet for another moment, letting the pure joy of physical connection fill me. Then, gently, I let go. My hands slip from around his ankles, and brush across the bridges of his feet.

I pray for the physical memory of this moment to lodge forever in my heart and soul.

He reaches down, takes my hand and helps me up just as he did so long ago in that dusty square next to the temple wall. I feel young and full of joyful energy. I feel as if the world has just been re-created, as if The Almighty has actually established his kingdom here and now through Yeshua's life, death and resurrection and has pronounced, "It is good."

I alone am the first human witness to it all.

His breath is as sweet and pure as a baby's. His dark eyes shine and His face ripples with smiles. I cannot take my eyes off him. He shakes his head as if he's as delighted to see me happy as I am to see him alive. I feel welcomed back from the grave … when it is he who has destroyed death's grasp.

Suddenly the words of Isaiah come to me: *"For the mountains may depart and the hills be removed, but my steadfast love shall not depart from you, and my covenant of peace shall not be removed, says the Lord, who has compassion on you."*

Yes, his love fills me and his peace calms me. And I realize that our understanding of him and his mission was far too small. Far too limited. Far too weak. Yeshua has more than overcome Rome. He has overcome death itself, that proof of evil's reign.

He has left the grave behind and is going to the Father. I see more clearly now than ever before that He is our personal, human connection with The Almighty.

He has opened the door to this whole wide suffering world and ushered in the love-saturated, life-filled Kingdom of God. His resurrection proves his power over sin and death ... proves his love for us, all of us.

The magnitude of who he is and what he has done stuns me. I have never before felt so hopeful about the future

I gaze at him and realize that I will never again lose him. He is alive. Unbelievable, but true.

He raises his eyebrows, cocks his head and nods toward the city, as if to say, "Well, Mary, be off, carry my message. I've made you my personal evangelist. Go share the good news."

My lips part to say, "Yes Rabonni, I'm on my way." Or "I shall always do your bidding."

But, there is no need. I simply nod. Then I take a step backward away from him and toward Jerusalem. I dare not take my eyes off him. Carefully I take another backward step, and another, and another. I'm backing my way toward Jerusalem because I dare not lose sight of Him.

He watches, clearly amused. And I love that.

As I carefully walk backward, he begins to change, to glow, bright as the morning sun. At first it looks like a waterfall of sunlight is pouring over him, gilding his hair and shoulders, until he's glimmering and shimmering. Then, it's like the sun-bright light is actually coming from within him, radiating from his eyes, shining from the palms of his hands, which he holds out toward me in blessing, and then the light blazes through every pore of his being, swirling around him sparkling in all colors imaginable. His luminous brilliance increases until he simply vanishes in the light. He is the light. Like the pillar of light that led our ancestors through the desert. Even as he grows brighter, his physical image softens airily until he simply disappears.

I stare with all my might at where he stood, trying to hold on to his form, to grasp some physical remnant of him . . . but there is nothing except pure, sunlit air.

And yet I know he lives.

With grateful heart, I cover my face in prayer and all I can say is, "Thank you! Thank you!"

And all my pain, all my fear and confusion, all my anguish is gone. Washed away in his light, in the reality of his being. Joy floods me. The world is brand new. Yeshua the Messiah lives. And the kingdom of God is at hand.

Turning toward Jerusalem, I feel radiant with thanksgiving. The fresh, clear air fills my lungs. The blessed truth nearly bursts off my tongue. I laugh out loud. I have seen the Lord and he is alive.

Yeshua is not dead!

He Lives!

This statement and promise from Yeshua is recorded in John 11: 25-26:

"I am the resurrection and the life;
He that believeth in me,
though he were dead,
yet shall he live;
and whosoever liveth and believeth in me
shall never die."

AUTHOR'S NOTE

....

Although this book is fiction, the experiences described imaginatively are biblically based. I invite you to read the biblical passages that inspired this book and allow your own imagination to expand your understanding.

The mourning song can be found in Jeremiah 9: 17-19

The story of men wanting to stone a woman caught in adultery can be found in John 8:3-11 (King James Version). Some other translations have it in John 7:53-58. Some translations list the story at the end of the book of John under the title, "An incident in the temple."

Jesus' baptism story can be found in Matthew 3:13-17, Mark 1:9-11 and Luke 3:21-22

The wedding feast at Cana story can be found in John 2: 1-11

The healing of Peter's mother-in-law story can be found in Matthew 8:14-15, Mark 1:29-31 and Luke 4:38-39.

The story about healing the woman suffering from a 12-year hemorrhage can be found in Matthew 9:18-26, Mark 5:21-34 and Luke 8:40-48.

The parable of the prodigal son can be found in Luke 15:11-32.

The story of the woman who had been bent over for 18 years can be found in Luke 13:10-17

The story of feeding the 5,000 with five barley loaves and two fish is the only miracle story found in all four gospels: Matthew 14:13-21, Mark 6:30-44, Luke 9:12-17, and John 6:1-13.

The story of anointing Jesus' feet with spikenard can be found in Matthew 26:6-13, Mark 14:3-9 and John 12:1-7

Reports of Jesus' crucifixion can be found in Matthew 27:33-50, Mark 15:22-37, Luke 23:33-46 and John 19:17-30

The story of the empty tomb can be found in Matthew 28:1-10, Mark 16:1-8, Luke 24:1–11 and John 20:1-18

QUESTIONS FOR DEEPER STUDY

Sometimes an old familiar story can feel new again when told in a fresh or unique way.

How did this story of the Promised One feel different as it was told through the voices of women?

What insights did you gain from this telling? Do you think these insights might change your view of yourself? Of your relationship with Jesus? Of your relationship with the church?

Let's consider how you might apply those insights to your life. These questions may help you.

Chapter 1: What Now?
Reports of Yeshua's crucifixion can be found in Matthew 27:33-50, Mark 15:22-37, Luke 23:33-46 and John 19: 17-30

1. Have you experienced a morning like what's described here? Where you wake up, and then suddenly remember some horror like the death of a friend, or the start of a war? If so, how did you get through the day?

2. Does this woman's response to trauma ring true to you?

Chapter 2: He Saved My Life

The story of men wanting to stone a woman caught in adultery can be found in John 8:3-11 (King James Version). Some other translations have it in John 7:53-58. Some translations list the story at the end of the book of John under the title, "An incident in the temple."

1. In this story of sin and righteousness, why do you think Yeshua's response to "the incident" differed from everyone else's response?

2. How did Yeshua's answer to the demand for punishment change the atmosphere?

3. In your life, would his statement, "The one who is without sin should cast the first stone," stop you in your judgmental tracks? And if so, why and how?

4. What insights can we gain from Yeshua's response to the self-righteous crowd?

5. What can we learn from his response to the woman?

6. How do the themes of law, justice, and mercy play out in this story?

Chapter 3: The Morning After

The experiences in this chapter can be seen as a story of women trying to make sense of their heart-wrenching grief. They gather in the traditional women's way — bearing food for comfort and sharing stories to keep memories alive.

1. How did these followers of The Promised One deal with their shared trauma?

2. Why is it important to gather when there is suffering?

3. What role does the sharing of food play in easing suffering?

4. Why do you think it was important for these women to share their experiences?

5. Have you ever taken part in a gathering like this? Why not share your story.

6. What does such sharing do for the story teller?

7. What do such stories do for the listener?

8. In today's world, can the sharing of food and personal memories hold the same healing powers for someone struggling with the loss of a dearly loved one?

Chapter 4: Mourning Together

The story about healing the woman suffering from a 12-year hemorrhage can be found in Matthew 9:18-22 (King James Version & New English Bible), Mark 5:21-34 (KJV & NEB), and Luke 8:40-48. The parable of the prodigal son can be found in Luke 15:11-32.

Dealing with chronic pain and illness is nearly unbearable. The woman in this story was so desperate that she disobeyed social and religious laws to seek healing. And yet, Yeshua did not criticize or correct her for her brazen behavior. Instead of censure, he says (for all to hear) it is her faith which has healed her.

1. What do we learn about the woman who touched Yeshua's garment?

2. What might be today's expression of faith when desperate for healing?

3. What insight can we gain from Yeshua's response to feeling that someone touched him?

4. If you had been in the crowd, how might you have responded to Yeshua's question, "Who touched me?"

5. Have you or anyone you know experienced healing in response to desperate faith action?

6. What do you think he means by the statement that her faith has healed her?

7. Why do you think he made such a public pronouncement about her faith and her healing, instead of simply saying "be healed" as he did with others?

Chapter 5: Surprise at the Goat Pasture

The story of Jesus' baptism can be found in Mark 1: 9-11, Matthew 3: 13-17, and in Luke 3: 21-22.

The wedding feast at Cana story can be found in John 2: 1-11

The story of feeding the 5,000 with five barley loaves and two fish can be found in

Matthew 14:13-21, Mark 6:30-44, Luke 9:12-17, and John 6: 1-13.

1. Why was it important that John baptize Jesus?

2. Did you realize that all three members of the Trinity appeared at his baptism: Jesus, the Son. The Holy Spirit in the form of a dove. The Father speaking his approval from heaven. What does this tell you about Jesus' baptism?

3. Jesus' first miracle took place at a wedding, where he changed water into wine so the feast could continue successfully. Why do you think he chose to make this his first miracle?

4. What part did his mother, Mary, play in this first miracle of his? And what can we learn from that?

5. Why do you think Jesus chose to perform a miracle and feed thousands from five small barley loaves and two fish, rather than simply send the people home?

6. What lessons did the disciples learn from this event? What lesson did the woman learn? What lessons do you think Jesus wanted them to learn?

Chapter 6: Dinner Party at Bethany

The story of anointing Jesus' feet with Spikenard can be found in Matthew 26:6-13, Mark 14:3-9 and John 12:1-7

1. Why do you think the disciples criticized the woman for giving Yeshua such a lavish gift? What do you think their motivation was?
2. Why do you think Yeshua speaks up on behalf of the woman? What is he trying to teach his disciples? What is he trying to teach her?
3. Do you identify with the disciples' disapproval of how the woman spent her money? Do you sometimes find yourself criticizing how others spend their money?
4. Do you identify with the woman, being criticized when you are trying to do something good? If so, do the words of Yeshua give you comfort? In what way?

Chapter 7: The Tomb

1. Have you gone to the cemetery on Memorial Day to pay your respects, or to decorate the graves of relatives? If so, what was that like for you?

2. How would you have reacted, if the grave you went to was open and the casket gone? Or the grave and casket were both open, and no body in sight?

3. Why do you think the angels quoted Yeshua to these grieving women?

4. Why do you think the disciples in hiding rejected the women's story?

5. What does it mean to you that Yeshua rose from his grave?

6. Why do you think Yeshua revealed his resurrection to Mary first?

In general:

1. Did you identify with any of these women, their experiences, their personal struggles, their life-changing encounters with Yeshua?

2. As you read through these stories of Yeshua's interaction with women, his statements to them or to others about them, his appearing first to Mary and commissioning her to tell his disciples that he'd risen from the dead, did you gain a new respect for the role women played in Yeshua's life and ministry?

3. Did Yeshua's treatment of women affect your view of yourself? If so, how?

4. Were you surprised that the women stayed all day at the crucifixion, and remained until they saw where his body was intomed? What does such loyalty (even in the face of danger) say about the women? What does it say about the Promised One?

5. Many of the religious leaders in Jerusalem approved of Yeshua's execution. What explains that? They had been studying their scriptures and watching for the coming Messiah for generations, and yet when the Messiah arrived they did not recognize him, approve of his message, or follow him. In fact, they wanted him dead. What lessons can we glean from this awareness (or lack of awareness)?

To learn more about Yeshua the Nazarene, read the four gospels of the New Testament. While each gospel emphasizes different aspects of his words and actions, together they provide the most comprehensive view of his earthly life.

Made in United States
Cleveland, OH
21 April 2025

16274421R00097